The Walking Trees

The Walking Trees
and Other Scary Stories

Roberta Simpson Brown

August House Publishers, Inc.
LITTLE ROCK

Published by August House, Inc.,
P.O. Box 3223, Little Rock, Arkansas, 72203,
501-372-5450.

Printed in the United States of America

10 9 8 7 6 5 4 3 2 1

LIBRARY OF CONGRESS CATALOGING-IN-PUBLICATION DATA

Brown, Roberta Simpson, 1939-
The walking trees : and other scary stories / Roberta Simpson Brown — 1st ed.
p.   cm.
Summary: Twenty-one contemporary scary stories, intended for reading aloud.
ISBN 0-87483-143-1 (alk. paper) : $7.95 tpb
1. Supernatural—Juvenile fiction. 2. Children's stories, American.
[1. Supernatural—Fiction. 2. Short stories .]
I. Title.
PZ7.B816923Wa l 1991
[Fic]—dc20   91-23759

First Edition, 1991

Executive: Liz Parkhurst
Project editor: Judith Faust
Design director: Ted Parkhurst
Cover design: Wendell E. Hall
Typography: Lettergraphics, Little Rock

This book is printed on archival-quality paper which meets the
guidelines for performance and durability of the Committee on
Production Guidelines for Book Longevity of the
Council on Library Resources.

AUGUST HOUSE, INC.   PUBLISHERS   LITTLE ROCK

To all my family, especially my husband, Lonnie;
to all the animals I love, especially Howard, Zeke, Inky, and Tuff;
and to all my kindred spirits in this world and the next

Acknowledgments

*T*hanks to my parents, Milton Tom and Mamie Lillian Simpson, for giving me a special life to write about.

To my sister Fatima Atchley for her music and stories and her willingness to listen to all I write.

To Myrtie Gaskins Sullivan, a great teacher and friend, who taught me to appreciate art, literature, and life.

To Charlie, Vicki, and Howard Brown, who inspired some of these stories.

To Charlene Cornell, Michael Cotter, John Ferguson, Tom Friedman, Mary Hamilton, Deanna Hansen, David Holt, Dolores Jackson, Reda King, Norma Lewis, Gail Moody, Elizabeth Rogers, Suzi Schuhmann, Georgia Wallace, Billy Edd Wheeler, Debbie Whyte, and many more who took time to give me support and good advice.

To Lee and Joy Pennington and all the members of the International Order of E.A.R.S., Inc., for giving me the opportunity to tell my stories.

And especially to my husband, Lonnie, who always takes time from his golf game to be there when I need him.

Contents

The Ticket Taker

Chrissy Chism tugged at her mother's arm as they left the ticket window and crossed under the banner welcoming them to the state fair.

"Mommy, let's go through that line," said Chrissy. "David's taking tickets."

"Who's David?" asked Denise Chism, looking down at her daughter.

"He's the man who took tickets at the Water Carnival," Chrissy said.

"No, honey," said her mother. "I doubt that he'd be way out here. Even so, how do you know his name? You know you're not supposed to talk to strangers."

"But he was nice, Mommy," Chrissy explained. "He talked to me while we were waiting for the ambulance for Trisha. He must have been scared about her, because his face was white. He told me not to worry, though. He said I'd see her again, but I didn't."

Denise Chism couldn't remember seeing anyone talking to Chrissy at the Water Carnival, and this disturbed her. What if he had been a child molester? She hadn't seen him, and he had gotten close enough to talk to her daughter.

"Chrissy, did anything else happen?" she asked.

"He just said he liked to visit with everybody," replied Chrissy.

Denise felt a little relieved. Maybe he hadn't singled Chrissy out. Maybe with everything happening so fast that night, he was just trying to comfort the frightened children in the crowd. It was probably part of his job. Still, it was odd that she couldn't remember seeing him.

She thought she remembered everything about that time.

It was the last vacation they had taken together as a family before the divorce. The days at the lake resort were supposed to make things better, but they hadn't. The only good thing was that the people in the next cottage had a daughter, Trisha, who was the same age as Chrissy, and the two families had become friends.

They had all gone to the Water Carnival together. When they bought their tickets, nobody had a hint of the terrible thing that was about to happen. Chrissy and Trisha had sat side by side, excited by the colored lights and the speed and spectacle of the boat show.

Then, without warning or apparent reason, one of the boats veered toward the shore and exploded. Flames and debris shot into the sky and seemed to hang suspended. Not everything went up, though. A small fragment from the engine soared like a missile toward the spectators along the shore. Nobody saw it coming until it had pierced Trisha's eye. She fell dead with a single, simple cry while they all stared in disbelief.

It wasn't likely that Denise Chism would ever forget that. It could so easily have been Chrissy.

By now they were near the state fair entrance, and several people crowded in ahead of Chrissy and Denise.

Chrissy stretched around the lady in front of them and yelled, "Hi, David! Remember me?"

Denise saw the man turn and look in their direction. The look gave her a strange feeling. Now, seeing him this close, she felt as if she *had* met him somewhere. For some reason, there were vague, fearful feelings associated with him. Maybe it was at the lake. That must have been where she had seen him. He probably worked for some company that produced shows, and they must have some of their shows on the midway. That would explain why he was here.

Though she continued to reason with herself, she was still afraid. She did not want this man near Chrissy. As the gates opened and the crowd surged forward, she yanked Chrissy to another line, gave the ticket taker their tickets, and hurried Chrissy along toward the midway. She couldn't help glancing over her shoulder to see if the man was following them. She was unnerved to find him looking at her with an amused smile.

"Mommy, slow down. You're walking too fast!" Chrissy protested.

Denise told herself she was being ridiculous. Nobody was following them, and nobody was going to hurt them in the middle of the crowded midway.

She smiled at Chrissy and bought a roll of bright red tickets for the rides and shows.

They rode the merry-go-round and the bumper cars, and then Chrissy raced for the Ferris wheel. Denise looked up and felt her stomach begin to churn. It was times like this she hated being divorced. Chrissy's father had always taken her on the rides. Now Denise would have to do it. She couldn't deprive Chrissy of fun just because she was afraid.

Denise was relieved when she saw that the ticket taker at the Ferris wheel was a woman. She sat beside Chrissy in the seat and made sure the bar was fastened securely. Then the big wheel turned, and they went up, up, and over.

As they came down, Denise thought back to when she was a little girl like Chrissy. She had loved the high rides, too. That had all changed one night when she rode the Ferris wheel with her best friend. The ride had upset Denise's stomach, and she didn't feel like getting on the carnival swings. Her friend did, though, and the swings went up and out, around and around, faster and faster. Suddenly, one broke, and Denise watched it go hurling through the air. When it landed, she ran over with everyone else. They said it was her friend, but Denise saw nothing familiar about the smashed mass lying on the ground. She'd been terrified of high rides ever since.

That had to be the reason she was so scared tonight. Chrissy had mentioned Trisha's death, and it had made her remember her own loss. She was glad when the ride was over and they were walking down the midway again.

She felt weak and shaky. She began to realize it wasn't because of the ride. She was experiencing a deep, unshakable foreboding. She kept seeing David's face. What was it that bothered her about that face? She couldn't figure it out.

"Chrissy, Mommy's not feeling well," she said. "I think it's time we went home."

"Please let me do one more thing!" pleaded Chrissy. "I've got one more ticket left."

They were near the end of the midway now, where the rides gave way to other attractions.

"Well, all right." Denise agreed reluctantly. "Use your last ticket, but pick something on the ground."

They were standing in front of the House of Mirrors. "How about this?" she asked Chrissy.

Chrissy was about to say yes, but something at the very end of the midway caught her eye.

"Look, Mommy! Look!" cried Chrissy. "I want to go there! Where David's taking tickets!"

Chrissy ran toward the tent. Denise saw David look at Chrissy and smile. For a second, she saw his face in the lights. Suddenly it all came back. It was impossible, of course, but she knew where she had seen that face. A man with a white face had taken her friend's ticket on the swings. Oh, no! She had forgotten. And Chrissy said the man at the Water Carnival the night Trisha was killed had had a white face. It couldn't be the same man after all these years. She had to be wrong, but she knew she wasn't.

She ran after Chrissy, but the little girl had a head start. Chrissy reached the tent, and the ticket taker smiled and took the ticket and tore it in half.

"No! Chrissy, no!" screamed Denise.

She tried to run faster, but her ankle twisted and she fell to the ground. She could see a sign above the tent blinking *"WELCOME TO GHOSTLAND."*

The pain blotted everything out, and she closed her eyes. When she opened them, people were standing around. A large man bending over her told her he was the manager of the midway shows and that a doctor was coming.

"You'll be fine," he said.

"Forget about me," she begged. "Please, my daughter. Your ticket taker, the one called David, took her into that 'Ghostland' tent show. Please get her. There's something strange about that man."

Denise struggled to sit up, and the manager tried to calm her.

"Take it easy, lady. You've had a bad fall," he said. "I'm sure your daughter is around here somewhere."

"I told you where she is!" Denise yelled.

"That's not possible," the manager said. "We don't have a ticket taker named David, and we've never had a show called 'Ghostland.'"

"It's there," she said, pointing to the end of the midway. "I saw it just before I fell."

She got up, pushing at the hands trying to restrain her. The weight on her ankle hurt terribly, and for a few seconds, everything turned black again. Then her panic brought strength, and she began to hop toward the field.

The manager took hold of her arm to give her support. The crowd moved as one silently behind them. She looked ahead and couldn't believe what she was seeing.

The field was empty. There was no tent or blinking sign. There was no little girl or white-faced ticket taker. They had vanished as completely as if the green grass had swallowed them up.

She stood staring, and they urged her to leave, to come with them. Arms pulled at her gently, and voices murmured that everything would be all right. She turned to go, but something on the ground caught her eye. She reached down slowly and picked it up. It was the torn half of a bright red ticket.

Bedtime Snack

*T*he creature lay on its back and floated in the water. If the light could have filtered down, it would have shown a dark mass just at the surface—a dark mass with two small, shiny eyes and a large, loose-lipped mouth that drooled hungrily.

The creature had started out small, but as it moved from place to place to find food, it grew to about the size of an inflated inner tube. It had found that it could inflate and deflate itself at will. It was at full form now, with its sleek, slimy skin stretched tight.

It moved and bobbed against the wood that extended along the water's edge. There was something familiar about that wood, but its sluggish brain couldn't quite figure out what it was. It would eat, deflate slowly into sleep, and drift to the wooded edge of the water. It would attach itself there, for how long it didn't know. Then it would experience the sensation of being out of the water completely, with the wind blowing over it. It would feel itself moving, but it had no idea how it was transported. Then it would wake up, refreshed and hungry, inflated in the water again. It didn't know where each snack came from, but it didn't worry. A snack always came—and it always came late at night.

It was late at night when Fran Miller unlocked the door of her house and hurried up to her room. The game had gone into overtime, and then her friends had wanted something to eat. Time had gotten away from her. She was glad her folks were asleep because it was past her curfew.

She usually didn't stay out late. Being out alone at night frightened her since the killings. She shuddered, remembering the pictures of those mutilated bodies splashed across the front page of the *City News*.

She told herself she probably had nothing to worry about. The last killing had been three weeks ago. She remembered because she had heard the men at the used-furniture store talking about it when Dad took her there to buy some different furniture for her room.

She tried not to think about the killings. She was tired now. All she wanted was a hot bath and a good night's sleep. There was nothing to be afraid of, yet she felt frightened. All her senses combined to send her the insistent message that something evil was lurking nearby—something nameless and sinister and deadly.

Fran dropped her clothes to the floor and crossed to the bath. Her ears picked up a low creaking sound. She stopped and listened. The sound did not come again.

"All old houses creak," she said to herself.

She ran the water hot and lay soaking away the tiredness. Then she heard it again—that low creaking sound, low but close. She strained to hear, but the house was silent. She stepped out of the tub, patted her skin dry with a soft towel, and slipped on her gown. Still uneasy, she hurried across the room and slid under the covers on her waterbed.

She liked to let the gentle movement of the bed lull her to sleep. She began to relax, feeling the water move back and forth. Suddenly she heard the low creaking sound again, and she realized that something odd was happening. The movement wasn't slowing down. It was growing. She could hear the water sloshing beneath her. She grabbed for the wooden sides of the bedframe to pull herself up.

There was a ripping sound, and Fran plunged into the water. Something slimy touched her hand. She screamed as loose, drooling lips closed around her arm. After that, the only sounds were the creaking of the bed and the churning of the water.

The morning edition of the *City News* carried the story of another strange killing, and the police continued their search for the killer.

A few days later, the truck from the used-furniture store pulled up in front of the home of the late Fran Miller. As they loaded her furniture, neither of the men noticed the dark mass attached to the wooden frame of the water bed. They drove away, and the wind and the movement roused the creature. It remembered—the wood, the wind, and the water. It snuggled down to sleep, for it knew that soon it would be back in the water, hungry for another bedtime snack.

Snowman

*T*he snow covered the trees and the fields and the farmhouse like white sheets covering the dead.

Jim and Helen Morris stood looking out the window watching their son, Travis, building a snowman. They agreed it had been a good idea to spend some time here at the farm Uncle Lightel had left them. They hoped maybe it would change Travis. He'd been so unruly until just lately.

Of course, there were some things that still bothered them about their son. Like right now, for instance: he was building the snowman on the exact spot where Uncle Lightel had died in that blizzard. The neighbor who found the old man said he was so covered with snow he looked like a snowman.

As Jim and Helen stood looking out, the wind picked up the snow and whirled it in an eerie dance.

"Look!" shouted Travis. "The snowman is dancing!"

And as they watched through deepening shadows, it really did look like the snowman had come to life.

The wind stopped as abruptly as it had started. The snow fell back to earth, showering Travis with big, wet flakes. He brushed them off and reached down and scooped up a handful of snow from the base of the snowman and began shaping it into a ball.

"You're getting your clothes wet," Helen called to her son. "Put that snowball down and come inside."

Travis went down the steps and opened the basement door, but he was still carrying the snowball in his hand. He could feel it tingling through his glove.

As he passed the freezer, he opened the lid and dropped the snowball inside. As he turned to go upstairs, his foot bumped against a pair of old snow boots by the freezer. He was puzzled. He didn't remember seeing them before. They must have belonged to Uncle Lightel.

He hurried upstairs to see what his mother was fixing for dinner.

"Travis," she said as he came into the kitchen, "would you please set the table for me? I'm going down to the freezer and get a package of pork chops for supper."

Travis thought of the snowball. She'd yell at him if she saw it in the freezer.

"I'll get the pork chops for you, Mom," he offered sweetly. "You don't need to run up and down those stairs."

"Why, thank you, dear," Helen said.

She was surprised. It was not like Travis to be so thoughtful.

When he reached the freezer, Travis looked down at the old snow boots again.

"That's funny," he thought. "I could swear those boots were turned the other way just a minute ago."

He opened the freezer lid, picked up a package of pork chops, and looked down at the snowball. He blinked and looked again. He must be seeing things. The snowball had a face. It had eyes, and a nose, and a mouth that was grinning up at him. He dropped the lid and raced up the stairs, taking two steps at a time.

All through supper that night, Travis thought about what had happened.

"Dad," he asked, "do you believe in ghosts?"

"Of course not," Jim answered.

"Well," said Travis, "I was just thinking that Uncle Lightel said he never wanted to leave this place. Do you think he could still be here?"

"Don't be silly," his mother told him. "Now, eat your supper before it gets cold."

Travis decided that this was not a good time to tell them about a snowball with a face and snow boots that turned by themselves. And he thought that, just to make sure it hadn't been his imagination, he would sneak down to the basement for another look before he went to bed.

After dinner, Travis waited until his father was reading and his mother was doing the dishes, and then he slipped down the hall and eased down the basement stairs.

He stumbled against something on the bottom step. He looked down. There were the snow boots, touching his foot.

He nearly bolted back up the stairs, but he didn't. His mom or dad must have come down and moved the boots without his knowing. He crossed over to the freezer, hesitated only a second, and raised the lid.

He had been right! It wasn't his imagination. The face on the snowball was looking up at him, and something about it was familiar.

Before he could move, the snow and frost in the freezer blew up and swirled around his face. He struggled to breathe in the cold. He tried to close the lid, but it was stuck. He heard footsteps crossing the basement and saw the snow boots beside him. He felt his body growing numb as the snow and frost engulfed him. Then the freezer lid clicked shut, and all was silent and cold and dark.

The boy crossed the basement carrying the snow boots and slowly climbed the stairs.

As he walked by the living room door, Jim asked, "What on earth have you been doing in the basement?"

"I found these old snow boots down there by the steps today. I wanted to put them away before someone tripped on them."

"That was very thoughtful of you, son," Jim told him. "You'd better go on to bed now."

The boy walked on, but he stopped in the hallway. Jim and Helen exchanged glances when he was out of sight.

"I've never seen such a change," said Helen. "He's acting so grown up! He even *looked* older just now."

"Yes," Jim said. "I think we ought to stay on here."

The boy smiled as he went on down the hall to his room. He was glad they were going to stay. He never wanted to leave.

Outside, the snowman stood silent, and the wind whirled the snow around him in an eerie dance.

Downstairs, the freezer kicked on, and a new layer of frost and snow formed over the snowball—like white sheets covering the dead.

Shadows

*T*he house stood shrouded in shadows, silent and still. Gladys Bates stood in the living room wondering if she and her husband Ben had made a mistake in buying the old house. She'd felt uneasy from the first time they'd looked at it, and she didn't know why.

It was a perfect place for the children. Little B.G. and Michelle could have their own rooms and a big, shady yard to play in. And the price had certainly been right. In fact, she couldn't believe it had been priced so low. Anyway, it was too late to back out now—even if they wanted to—because the moving men had just unloaded the van and driven away.

She had set about unpacking. Ben lit a fire in the big fireplace and went off for a meeting with a client. B.G. and Michelle had raced off to explore the other rooms, and Gladys stood looking at all the boxes she still had to unpack.

She moved closer to the fire. She couldn't get warm. The house seemed unusually cold.

Gladys shivered as B.G. and Michelle came running into the room.

"Mommy!" they shouted. "Come see the shadows in our room. They're holding hands."

An old fear, long-forgotten, flashed through her mind. There was an old Simon and Garfunkel song called "Bleeker Street." It had been a favorite of her mother's years ago. As a child, Gladys had been frightened by the line about a shadow holding a shadow's hand. She used to lie awake at night afraid that the shadow's hands would touch her.

She looked down at her little girls, and she could see that they were frightened, too.

"There's nothing to be afraid of," she told them. "Shadows don't hold hands."

"These do," B.G. insisted.

"You're only seeing tree limbs outside your window," Gladys explained.

"No, Mommy," said Michelle. "These are people shadows."

"Yeah," B.G. added, "and they said they're hungry. They want cookies and milk."

Gladys smiled.

"Oh," she said. "I'm beginning to get the picture. Shall I fix a tray of cookies and milk for you to take to your room?"

"Yes, Mommy, that would be nice," Michelle said solemnly.

"Please hurry, Mommy," said B.G. "The shadows don't like to wait."

A few minutes later, Gladys watched her two small girls climb the stairs carrying the cookies and milk. She went back to her unpacking.

"Those two are turning into real little con artists," she said to herself. Ben would enjoy hearing about this little episode when he got home.

At 8:30, Gladys decided to take a break and go tuck B.G. and Michelle in for the night. She expected to find them playing with their toys, but instead, she found them huddled together on the floor with the empty tray in front of them.

"Mommy," B.G. said in a small, frightened voice, "the shadows were mean to us. They ate all our cookies and milk."

Michelle looked up, her voice almost a whisper as she spoke.

"Could we have some more, Mommy? The shadows are still hungry."

Gladys was puzzled. The girls had never acted this way before.

"You've had enough, girls," she said. "If the shadows are hungry, they'll just have to wait until breakfast like the rest of us. Now hop in your beds so I can tuck you in."

"Mommy, can I sleep with Michelle tonight?" asked B.G. "I don't like the shadows."

Gladys looked around the room. She could see spooky shadows moving along the wall. She didn't like them either, so she smiled at the two little serious faces.

"OK," she said. "You may sleep together, but just for tonight."

She kissed them both goodnight and went back downstairs to continue unpacking. She worked until just before time for Ben to come home. She stopped and made some sandwiches and coffee.

When she heard his car pull into the drive, she crossed the hall to open the door for him. She heard the children cry out. She listened, but she didn't hear them again.

"This new place must be giving them bad dreams," she thought. "I'll check on them before we go to bed."

As she and Ben ate their sandwiches and drank their coffee, she told him about how she had been conned into fixing cookies and milk for hungry shadows. She thought he'd laugh, but instead, he looked at her rather oddly.

"What's wrong?" she asked.

"Well, it's probably nothing, but my client told me something horrible about this house tonight. He said the people who lived here before us abused their children. They locked them in a room upstairs and starved them to death."

Gladys didn't remember getting up. She just realized she was running up the stairs with Ben close behind her. They reached Michelle's room and threw open the door. Gladys sagged against Ben in relief. Both little heads were on the pillow, eyes peacefully closed.

Ben and Gladys walked arm-in-arm across the room and stood looking down at their two little girls.

Then, suddenly, shadows began to dance along the walls, and Ben and Gladys felt their blood chill. The room filled with great menacing shadows. They knew something was terribly wrong, and they yanked the cover from the children.

Both stood frozen in horror and disbelief. The sight was unspeakable. All the flesh had been gnawed from those little bones all the way up to their heads.

Ben and Gladys felt the shadows touch them, swirling and smothering their screams. Then all was darkness, and the house stood shrouded in shadows, silent and still.

Night Catch

The darkness was so thick that nothing could stir in it. The moon moved slowly out from behind a cloud and glared down at the earth like a cold, evil eye. Its light shone on two figures seated on the ground holding their nets.

"Can we go now?" asked the first. "I think we've got enough for a good meal."

"Let's wait a little longer," said the second. "I'd like to catch at least one more. They're really thrashing in the nets tonight."

So they sat and they waited.

In a nearby cottage, a small light flicked on.

One nudged the other. "Look at that little light," the nudger said. "It reminds me of catching fireflies when I was little."

"Me, too," said the other. "It's strange the things you remember."

They both chuckled.

In that nearby cottage, Linda Marshall was not laughing. She was trying to figure out why her mom and

dad had thought this God-forsaken place would be good for a family vacation. All she and her brother Roy had done since they got here was fight.

It was great for Mom and Dad—*they* spent all their time at the club house—but it was boring for her and Roy without their friends.

Whenever Roy was bored, he always picked a fight. He had stormed out of the house again tonight after another argument, and she had cried herself to sleep on the couch.

But something woke her. It was a strange cry out there in the dark. It must have been an animal, but it sounded almost human.

She wished her mom and dad were home. She even wished Roy would come back. It made her nervous to be alone.

She paced back and forth, and as she paced, the thought came to her that maybe Roy couldn't come back. Maybe he had hurt himself. Maybe he was the one who had cried out in the dark. Something must be wrong. He should have been back long ago. She would have to go look for him. Her parents would ground her for life if she let anything happen to Roy.

She grabbed her jacket and went to the kitchen counter for the flashlight. It wasn't there. Roy must have taken it. She pulled back the curtain and looked out the window. There was just enough chilly moonlight for her to see the forms of nearby trees. She could see how to walk without the light.

She opened the door and stepped outside. She moved down the path in the direction Roy had gone. Everything was unnaturally still. Even her own footsteps barely made a sound.

"Roy?" she called. "Where are you?"

There was no answer.

She looked back at the house. She had come farther than she thought. Surely Roy had to be somewhere close. Maybe he'd doubled back to the house. Perhaps she should go back and check, and then go get Mom and Dad if he wasn't there yet.

She turned, and the toe of her shoe hit something and sent it rolling on the ground. She knelt and picked it up. It was Roy's flashlight. Now she really was frightened. He must be hurt.

She started to get up, but something fell across her face like a giant, stringy cobweb. She looked up to see two dark figures looming over her. She fought and thrashed as the net pulled tighter.

Another cry filled the night. This time it was hers.

The two figures grinned greedily at each other.

"Can we go now?" asked the first. "We've got enough for a good meal."

"Yes," said the second. "We have enough for tonight."

The moon was brighter now. It reflected from their white skulls and their green, moldy faces as they took their night's catch and sank slowly back into their graves.

Fish Bait

*T*he lapping against the dock was not a soothing sound. A splash in the murky water sent ripples scurrying to shore as if they were trying to get away from something. Chuck Bateman sat on the bank and watched the river nibble its way closer and closer to his campsite by the old deserted bait shop.

The wind rattled the faded "fish bait" sign just enough to make Chuck jumpy. Maybe his mom had been right. Maybe he should have stayed at the main lodge. It was beginning to look like it might rain tonight.

Of course, he couldn't just break camp and go back after insisting that he was old enough to camp out for one night alone. His dad had backed him up. Thirteen was old enough to take care of himself if his dad thought so. It was just that with the sun setting and the shadows filling the woods, he wasn't as sure as he had been that morning.

Those old men had started his uneasiness that afternoon.

Chuck hadn't had his line in the water long when they came up to him. He felt the tug at his baited hook about the time the two men sat down beside him on the bank.

He yanked hard, and the biggest catfish he'd ever seen came flying out of the water. It hovered above them for a second, and the huge eye on the right side of its head seemed to take in the entire scene near the dock. Then it flipped over, easily freeing itself from the hook, and fell back into the river.

"Good Lord!" Ed Smitty said. "Did you see that fish?"

"I saw it, all right. It was Old Whiskers himself," replied John Stevens. He shook his head. "Boy," he said, "do you know what you've done?"

"Let the biggest fish I ever saw get away," Chuck answered, angry and disappointed.

He wanted to add that it might not have happened if they hadn't come up and distracted him, but he knew it wouldn't do any good to say it now.

"The fella that used to own that bait shop caught Old Whiskers one time. He should have thrown him back right away. That old catfish belongs in the river," Ed Smitty declared.

"Yep," John Stevens agreed. "There's something un-natural about that fish. Something bad happens to everybody that even hooks him."

"Yep," echoed old Smitty. "Jim Ford never did get that fish mounted on his wall. Lost his eye on a fish hook right after he hooked Old Whiskers. He just closed the bait shop and moved away."

Chuck shut out most of the stories. He was glad when the superstitious old men left. There was no way to reason with them. Besides, his dad and mom didn't allow him to talk back to his elders.

There was another loud splash near the dock as the two men sputtered off in John's ancient truck.

Smitty leaned out the window and yelled, "Watch out for Old Whiskers tonight, Chuck!"

Chuck could see them laughing as they turned the bend. He watched them out of sight, and he had a sudden urge to call them back. All at once, he was filled with foreboding, and he didn't want to be alone.

The only thing he knew to do was to keep busy.

Thunder rumbled in the west as Chuck cooked supper. He looked up at the cloud just as a dark form splashed out of the water and fell back again. He couldn't see it clearly, but it was as big as they'd said Old Whiskers was.

The rain came just as he finished eating. He crawled in his tent, thinking that the rain would bring up lots of night crawlers. He pulled his sleeping bag around him and went to sleep.

He'd slept about an hour when a sharp crack woke him. He couldn't tell if it had been a keen clap of thunder or a truck backfiring. He turned over, and his hand touched something wet and stringy. He flicked on his flashlight and saw a worm and three catfish whiskers on his sleeping bag. He knocked them off and sat there wondering how on earth they got in his tent. Then he remembered the sound that had waked him. It must have been John's truck. Those old jokers must have sneaked back and played a trick on him. They were probably outside laughing right now.

He turned the flashlight off and finally went back to sleep. No sound woke him this time, but he was sure there had just been one. It was too quiet. Cautiously, he reached out and felt around in the dark. He was relieved to find nothing there. He stretched his legs, and his foot touched something cold and wet.

He scrambled out of the sleeping bag and unzipped it all the way to the bottom. He grabbed his flashlight and directed the light to the bottom of the bag. He groaned, and his hand flew to his mouth. Gagging, he knocked the repulsive thing to the tent floor where it lay staring at him. It was a fish eye—a single fish eye looking up at him accusingly.

He opened the tent flap and kicked the eye as far as he could.

"Here's your fish eye, you clowns! The joke's over!"

He listened intently, but all he heard was the lapping water and rustling sounds among the blades of grass.

Frightened now, he stepped backward. His foot slipped and he fell, bringing the tent down on top of him. The rain coming in through the open flap beat steadily on his face. He couldn't put the tent back up in the storm, so he grabbed his flashlight and his sleeping bag and dashed to the old deserted bait shop.

Inside it was dirty and musty, but it was dry. He finally slept, and this time, it was an odor that woke him—not the musty odor he had smelled when he first came in, but the awful stench of dead, rotting fish.

He was furious. He could take a joke as well as the next guy, but this time those two old men had gone too far. He wouldn't turn on the light this time; he'd slip out and catch them red-handed.

He swung himself around to get up, but his feet came down on a floor that seemed to be squirming and moving.

He tried to get back into the bag, but he was carried across the room toward the door. He flung his arms wildly, and one hand grabbed the flashlight.

When the light came on, his mind struggled to process what he saw. The entire floor was covered with a moving mass of night crawlers carrying him along like a flattened escalator. The front door was open, and worms were falling off the hinges and casing onto the wriggling mass below.

His mouth flew open, but before he could scream, a sharp, pain ripped into his jaw and came out underneath. From the corner of his eye, he could see the gleam of a shiny fish hook sticking through the skin. Blood bubbled in his throat and dripped in little pools on the floor. He heard the splash again, and felt himself jerked through the air. He soared, and then it was he who splashed. He sank down, down in the murky water.

The waves lapped gently on the sand, leaving scallops of bloody pink foam. A huge dark form leapt joyously in the water and merged with the white mist of morning.

Around the bend, Ed Smitty and old John Stevens sputtered along with their day's supply of fish bait.

"Do you suppose it's over yet?" asked Smitty.

"Yep," said John. "It's over now. Young folks just don't listen, do they?"

Smitty shook his head.

The two men smiled and rode in silence. Fish would be biting good today with the river so full and happy.

Howard's Howling

The green mist rose from the pond and drifted across the field toward the house. Lee and Marsha Browning didn't see it because they were sleeping after an exhausting day of moving into their new house.

As the green mist floated closer, Howard woke in his place by the bed and looked toward the window. Though he couldn't hear anything, he knew something was out there. He threw back his little black head and howled such an unearthly howl that it jolted Lee and Marsha awake. They could hardly believe such a sound had some from such a small dog.

They looked out to try to see what had made him carry on so, but saw only the green mist shimmering in the moonlight. They figured Howard was just having trouble adjusting to night sounds in the country after living in a city condo.

The adjustment had been easy for Marsha and Lee. This place was just what they had always dreamed of— secluded and enchanting. There were trees and wild flowers and a pond down in the field. Howard had lots of room to run and explore.

Only one thing had bothered them about the place. The old man who sold them the land told them it was part of an ancient Indian burial ground. They might, he said, want to look through some documents that had been in his family for generations. He gave them a faded black box filled with yellowed papers.

After glancing at the old maps, they decided there were no graves on the site where they wanted to live. They built their house and moved in.

On the first night, Howard had started the eerie howling. It continued every night that week, and they couldn't figure out why. When they looked out, they saw only the green mist rising from the pond.

They noticed that Howard would not go with them when they walked by the pond. They noticed, too, that there were no other animals or birds near the banks.

The water was dark green and still, but it wasn't stagnant. It seemed to feed from an unknown source.

They were so happy to be in their new home that they gave it little thought.

Then one night they went to bed and were just drifting off to sleep when they heard a soft plop against the house. They listened, and they heard another soft plop against the window. It sounded like something wet—like a piece of fresh meat dropped on a counter.

Lee started toward the window to look out, but Howard flung himself in front of it, barking so furiously that Lee stopped. Lee saw the little dog was trembling, so he picked him up and held him until he stopped shaking. By the time Howard was calm, the noise had stopped.

Apparently, whatever had been out there was gone. Lee and Marsha went back to bed and heard nothing else that night.

When Lee woke in the morning, his first thought was to check outside. He opened the door and started to step out, but something on the doorstep caught his eye. He looked down. There was a circle of feathers on the step. He called Marsha to come see, but neither of them could figure out what it could mean. Howard couldn't have caught a bird; he'd been in the house all night. And he certainly wouldn't have arranged feathers in a circle.

"Maybe they're from an Indian headdress," Marsha teased. "Maybe we are on an Indian burial ground after all."

The day passed with the mystery unsolved. They tried to dismiss it as some animal just passing through, and they told themselves it was only a one-time thing.

That night, just after Lee and Marsha had gone to bed, the wet, plopping sound started again. They sat up and listened. It continued in a slow rhythm like a muffled drum.

"Tom-toms?" joked Lee, but neither one of them felt much like laughing.

Lee got up to cross to the window, but Howard began to howl again. Lee could tell it was too dark to see outside, but he thought perhaps he should go out and take a look. Again Howard blocked his way, and Lee was forced to reach down and lift the little dog from the floor. There was one more wet plop against the window, and then the noise stopped.

Marsha took Howard and put him in the bathroom. She followed Lee from the bedroom in time to see him turn on the porch light and open the door. He stood staring down at something, so Marsha crossed and stood behind him, looking over his shoulder.

There was something on the steps again. There were two bones neatly crossed. Howard couldn't have done that. He'd been inside with them. Besides, the only bones Howard ever touched were Milk Bones.

When morning came, they took a careful look around the house. There were spots on the outer walls and windows where something had hit, and there were traces of something slimy and green.

They were beginning to understand how Howard felt. They, too, were frightened. Lee decided to stay up that night and find out what was going on.

All that day, the green mist hung low over the pond. Lee and Marsha kept Howard inside. They sat at the kitchen table trying to figure out what the noise could be.

Marsha got out the faded black box with the yellowed papers that the old man had given them, and they searched through old documents and letters for some clue to explain what was happening.

As they were about to give up, Marsha found some hand-written papers in the bottom of the box. Someone had copied a legend. As they read, a gruesome tale unfolded.

The story spoke of a boneless evil that had stalked the Indians. Night after night, this boneless, green mass would attack the tepees and suck the bones from its victims. Finally, the old medicine man found a way to trap and hold the thing in a hole outside the village. He had the braves fill the hole with the bodies of animals and birds they had killed on their hunts, and when the evil thing began to eat, the old medicine man held it with a powerful magic spell. The braves filled in the hole, and as the earth sank down, a natural pond was formed, a watery covering for the grave where the green evil slumbered. No bird or animal would go near the place of the evil thing's burial, and each night, a warrior stood guard to warn the village in case the spell should be broken and the thing should wake.

Sitting there with the sunlight streaming through the kitchen window, Lee and Marsha decided one of their friends had heard the legend and was trying to scare them. That night, Lee stayed up to catch whoever was doing it.

Lee sat by the front door, and Howard and Marsha went to the bedroom. They were dozing off when the wet, plopping sounds started again. They got louder, and Howard began to howl. Marsha heard Lee open the door and go out. There was a thud and a choked-off cry. She heard nothing more except the plopping sounds.

As she started to get out of bed, something struck the window with a force that rattled the panes. She looked up, unable to believe what she was seeing. A huge green blob of something was hurling itself against her window. It wasn't being thrown; it was clearly throwing itself—and it was trying to get to her.

She screamed, and she managed to reach the phone and call the police.

"This is Marsha Browning on Green Pond Road. Please come quick. It's not just a pond. Don't think I'm crazy. I need help! The Indians buried something evil and boneless and green here. There's a warrior, they left a warrior to guard it, but he can't stop it. It's trying to get in my house! Please!"

45

The young officer who took the call could hear the plopping and howling in the background as she sobbed out her story. He was trying to make sense out of what she was saying about the pond and the ancient Indian burial ground when he heard the shattering of glass and a fierce cry that froze the blood in his veins.

Her voice came pleading through the howling and the sounds of struggle. "Please hurry!" she begged. "He's trying to protect me, but he's just not strong enough."

There was a thud, and then the line went dead.

Sirens shrieked and blue lights flashed by the pond with the green mist rising. The policemen jumped from the car and raced toward the house. They stopped abruptly when they reached the front door. On the doorstep lay a piece of skin with splintered bones sticking through it.

The two entered the house cautiously. In the bedroom, glass from the broken panes lay scattered on the floor. Wet streaks led from the bed to the window. The young officer punched his partner and pointed up. Buried in the wall above the bed was a tomahawk covered with green slime.

Who had she meant, he thought, when she said on the phone, "He's trying to protect me"? He'd thought it was the dog he heard barking in the background. But there was that shout, that... war cry.

The young officer shook his head. This is stupid, he thought. There couldn't have been an Indian here.

No, surely there couldn't have been a warrior there, an Indian trying to warn them that *this* burial ground was not a place where his people were buried; it was a place where they had buried the boneless, green, evil thing.

There couldn't have been a warrior trying to tell them with his feathers and bones that the nameless evil had broken the spell and that it had risen from its murky grave. No ghostly brave could have tried to kill a slimy thing with a tomahawk, could he?

The police found no trace of Lee or Marsha or the little black dog. They closed the house, and it still stands empty.

Sometimes at night, a lonely sound breaks the silence in that field by the pond. Some say it's a spirit dog calling its master, but some know that the green mist is rising hungrily and Howard is howling again.

The Walking Trees

*T*he campers had worked all afternoon setting up camp and gathering wood for the fire. Now the light from that fire was all the light they could see. The surrounding woods were dark, and the campers inched closer together as the ghost tales started.

The counselors had put Michael next to them near the campfire so they could keep an eye on him. He had already been in trouble several times that day—for loosening tent ropes, slipping snakes into sleeping bags, and putting frogs in water jugs. They'd put his friend Tim Garner beside him, hoping Tim would be a good influence. Tim never caused problems.

Michael sat quietly, but his mind seemed to be wandering, thinking of new tricks, no doubt. Tim listened to all the stories, but seemed especially to be absorbed in the one about the walking trees.

It was the story of a witch who once owned the forest with the little creek running through it where otters splashed and played. Flowers flourished along the banks, surprising nature lovers with unexpected color when they came to camp on the land.

The nature lovers left surprises for the witch, too. On her daily rounds, she found broken bottles, paper bags, beer cans, candy wrappers, and foul-smelling half-eaten food.

How this enraged her! She would swish around on her broom, fan the fire under her cauldron, and write NO TRESPASSING signs in bats' blood. Nothing helped. The campers took down the signs, tore them into little pieces, and scattered them along the trails. One day, as she was extracting a beautiful red maple leaf from a half-burned, gooey marshmallow, she decided she'd had enough.

"The next campers who clutter up my forest," she vowed, "will be sorry. I will turn them into trees so they will have to live in this mess."

Her chance came almost before she could gather the ingredients for her spell.

As she plucked the last wart from a toad, she saw a group of campers eating beside her little stream. Two chicken bones plopped into the water, splashing her skirt. An apple core landed by a tree, and bits of paper fell to the ground.

"Clean it up!" she screeched.

The intruders got up to go, calling over their shoulders, "Cool it, lady. It's no big deal. Who cares, anyway?"

"I do!" she yelled at their retreating backs, but their laughter mocked her as they continued down the path, giving no indication they would do as they were told.

She couldn't stand their indifference. She flung her arms toward the heavens and cried out her curse. The wind howled, and the earth opened up in a few selected places.

This stopped the retreaters in their tracks. Frightened now, they tried to run, but they discovered that they couldn't move. Their feet were becoming rooted in the openings in the earth, and their arms were turning to branches. Their cries filled the air and they begged for another chance.

"I want no more campers in my forest," she said. "For one night each year, I will give you the power to walk. Each year, on that night, you must stalk campsites and catch campers to replace you if you ever want to be free."

Horrified, they told her, "We could never do that."

"We'll see," she cackled, and off she flew.

The leaves fell and exposed the bare branches. The trees shivered, for their bark was thin and would not keep out the cold. Their suffering erased all traces of human-ness. All that mattered was to be free of the spell. Once each year, the trees walked…and captured campers to take their place in the witch's forest.

The story ended, and it was time for the boys to turn in.

"Those scary tales have got 'em all set up," said Michael when he and Tim were back in the tent they shared. "When they're all in bed, I'm going to sneak out in the woods and scare 'em pop-eyed."

"I don't think that's a good idea," said Tim.

"Why not?" challenged Michael.

"Well," whispered Tim, "it's just kind of scary. When that counselor told that story about the walking trees, I got the strangest feeling those trees out there were moving closer to the campfire."

"You're a big baby," sneered Michael. "Nothing out there is going to hurt you."

"I don't care. I'm not going. Besides, the counselors told us not to leave the tent," argued Tim.

"Then stay here and be a wimp," said Michael. "I don't need you anyway."

With that, he opened the tent flap and disappeared into the darkness.

Tim lay very still and listened. He could hear Michael's footsteps as he moved among the trees.

Suddenly he heard one sound: "*Ahhhaaack!*"

Then there was silence.

"He'll be back any minute now," thought Tim. "He'll roll around laughing all night about what he's done."

Tim waited, but nothing happened. He began to feel sleepy, so he snuggled down in his sleeping bag.

"To heck with him," Tim thought to himself. "He probably got caught and has to sleep with the counselors."

Tim found that idea funny as he drifted off to sleep. It must be storming, for he could hear a rumbling and the tent shook. Something was rubbing against the top of it, making a soft scratching sound.

"I get it," thought Tim. "He's raking something against the tent to scare me. Well, I'm not falling for that one."

When Tim woke, it was morning. He looked at Michael's sleeping bag. It was empty. He could still hear the soft scratching sound on top of the tent. He crawled over and looked out. He found himself staring at the trunk of a huge, ugly tree. The soft scratching sounded again and Tim looked up.

He thought at first he must be having a nightmare. A body that had actually become part of the branches was hanging head down, swaying back and forth, the fingers scratching the tent top.

For a moment, Tim couldn't move. He stared, hypnotized by the figure in the tree. There was no doubt about it. He recognized the face of his friend, Michael Barnes, even though the features were distorted by silent terror.

Panic struck. Tim whirled and faced the camp. The eerie silence seeped into his consciousness. There, in a ring of grotesque trees, hung all the others—all the counselors and campers dangling like broken limbs.

They were all dead. And the trees had done it. Somehow he knew. He tried to run, but it was too late. His feet were already becoming rooted to the earth and his arms were turning into branches.

Something heavy began to flow through his veins. Then he relaxed, and once again he was with all the others.

Rain Thing

*D*ana Anderson hated the rain. She'd felt that way ever since her mom and dad had bought the little farm by the woods that ran along Damron's Creek. The first rain drops would send her racing inside to hide in the corner as far from the door and windows as she could get.

This surprised her parents. She had enjoyed playing in the rain before they moved here.

"Why do you hate the rain?" they asked over and over.

Her answer was always the same. "The Rain Thing is out there in the woods by the creek, and it wants to get me."

Bill and Dee Anderson worried about the change in their daughter. They thought maybe she'd overheard some of the old-timers down at the little country store telling tales about strange happenings years ago along Damron's Creek, so they questioned her about the origin of the Rain Thing.

"I dream about it all the time," she explained. "It lives in Damron's Creek, and it only comes out and roams the woods when it rains."

Even though they asked her again and again, she could never tell them what the Rain Thing looked like.

"It's big and shadowy and dripping," she said. "And it's lonely."

Her parents couldn't convince her there was nothing out there. They tried to reason with her, but she resisted all their efforts.

Finally her father asked, "Why would the Rain Thing be after you? You haven't done anything to it."

"I told you," she insisted. "It doesn't want to be alone, so it tries to take me with it on dark, rainy nights."

Her father didn't know what else to do to comfort her, so he smiled and hugged her and promised, "Then we'll just have to stay with you on dark and rainy nights."

Dana was happy about that, yet way down deep inside, she was still afraid.

Dark and rainy nights came often that year. Dana would pace the floor and close the curtains and claim that the Rain Thing was out in the woods watching from the banks of Damron's Creek.

The weeks just before harvest brought hot, dry days, and Dana began to relax and play and look more like her old self. Bill and Dee Anderson began to hope that she had forgotten about the Rain Thing.

Then one day, clouds began to gather in the west, and rain threatened to come in by nightfall. Dana watched tensely as her father hurried to the fields and her mother hurried to the garden. They had work to finish before the storm broke.

Dana sat beside the creek skipping rocks. She saw her mother stop several times between the rows and wipe her brow. Suddenly, she heard her scream. Dana dashed across the yard as her mother came staggering from the garden.

"Run get your dad, Dana. Hurry, honey! Tell him a copperhead bit me."

Dana felt frozen, but her body was moving. Somehow she reached her father in the field and made him understand what had happened. Then he was running ahead of her toward the house.

By the time Dana caught up, her father was already bending over her mother, working frantically. He turned to Dana.

"I've done all I can," he said. "I've got to get her to the county hospital. I need you to stay here and feed the stock. I'll be back as soon as I can."

He picked up her mother and was gone before Dana had time to protest.

Time dragged by. The late afternoon sky was already dark, and Dana could feel the rain in the air. She went to the barn early and fed the animals, but the approaching storm made them as restless and uneasy as she was.

Back at the house, she tried to eat, but she wasn't hungry. She worried that her mother might die and she worried that her father might get caught in the storm. She tried to think about what she should do if she had to spend the night alone. She watched the clouds slip closer and closer.

The night and the rain came together, but her father did not come at all. She locked the door and closed the curtains, and she sat listening to the rain drumming on the metal roof. When she couldn't bear the waiting any longer, she pulled back the edge of the curtain and peeked out. She could see nothing but the drops of rain on the glass.

Nothing seemed to be moving, so she opened the window a little to see if she could hear some sign of her father.

"Who's gonna stay with me this dark, rainy night?" she said softly to herself.

She was startled to hear a faint voice answer from way back in the woods, "I will."

She slammed the window, locked it, and stood there trembling.

She wondered if it could possibly have been her father's voice answering her. Could the sound have carried on the water? Maybe he was coming along the creek in the woods and heard her.

She cautiously unlocked the window and raised it slightly again.

This time, she called directly into the darkness, "Who's gonna stay with me this dark, rainy night?"

From the middle of the woods, a voice answered more strongly, "I will!"

With the wind and the rain and the distance between them, Dana still couldn't tell if it was her father or not.

"Dad, is that you?" she called frantically.

There was no answer.

She leaned out to listen. She heard nothing but the rain. She wept silently, her tears blending with the raindrops on her cheeks.

"Who's gonna stay with me this dark, rainy night?" she cried.

From the very spot where the woods met the yard, a strange voice said loudly, "I will!"

Before she could move, a huge dripping, shadowy, faceless thing came floating toward her from the trees, and this time it wasn't a dream.

Dana never knew that her mother survived or that her father made it home safely. When he arrived, the door was still locked, but Dana had vanished.

Some people say that a shadowy form sometimes comes to the surface of Damron's Creek. Those who have been brave enough to go to the bank and look down into that water have seen deep into its eyes, and they swear that it has the face of Dana Anderson.

Lockers

Carol Hansen knew there was something strange about her new school the minute she walked in the door. She could feel an unseen presence staring at her as she walked down the hall. She thought the feeling would go away as she adjusted to her new schedule, but it didn't.

She noticed something else strange about her new school, too. Nobody was ever late. Students gathered by the water fountain or the restrooms or lockers would stop whatever they were doing when the tardy bell rang and hurry to class. Nobody stayed out after the final bell.

That amazed Carol. She couldn't believe anyone was that eager to get to class. She thought there must be a pretty stiff penalty for tardies. She would have to find out.

She found out sooner than she expected.

Carol stayed after her last class one afternoon to get some notes from her locker. She was busy sorting out what she needed for her report when she again had that odd feeling of being watched. She looked up and saw that the halls were deserted. Everyone had left at the last bell. She began to feel uneasy. She stuffed her books back in the locker, grabbed her notes, and hurried down the hall to the front door.

When she pushed it open and stepped out into the chilly afternoon air, she realized she'd left her jacket in the locker room. She knew she'd have to go get it. Her mother had just given her a lecture about being more responsible and keeping up with her things. She could imagine what would happen if she went home without her jacket.

She turned and hurried down the hall to the locker room. She reached out to push the door, but it burst open, and her friends Cindy and Betty came running out, nearly knocking her down.

"Run!" they yelled. "Run! Listen to the lockers!"

They ran on without looking back, and Carol stood staring in confusion. The door was open, and Carol could see her jacket inside on the bench right where she'd left it. Nothing was moving, but far back in the locker room, there was a faint banging sound coming from the lockers.

Carol knew she'd be in trouble if she went home without that jacket, but she seemed also to know she'd be in greater trouble if she went into the locker room alone. She turned and ran after her friends.

She thought they'd wait for her, but they didn't. They'd run down the hall and out the door without stopping.

"Well!" she said to herself, "I'll have a few things to say to those two tomorrow."

When tomorrow came, the first thing she had to do was retrieve her jacket from the locker room. Her mother had given her another lecture, but she had given her another chance, too. She made it clear, though, that if it ever happened again, she'd be grounded.

It was noon before she saw Cindy and Betty. They were in the cafeteria sitting at a table with some girls from P.E. class. She took her tray over and joined them.

"Hey!" she said, "what was the big idea of running out on me in the locker room yesterday?"

The girls exchanged looks, but didn't answer.

"Well? I'm waiting," she persisted.

Jason Evans and some of his friends were sitting at the next table listening.

"Tell her," sneered Jason.

The girls glared at him, but said nothing.

"Haven't you heard?" he continued. "This school is haunted."

Jason and his friends laughed nervously and got up to leave. Carol noticed they all stayed together.

She looked back at the girls. They had their heads down looking at the food they were pushing around on their trays. Carol waited. Cindy was the first to speak.

"Oh, all right," she said. "I guess you'll have to find out sooner or later. I might as well tell you. You see, it happened here at this school five years ago. A group of students were late for class, and as they walked by the locker room, they heard a scuffling noise inside. Since they weren't too eager to get to class anyway, they decided to go in and see what was going on. When they pushed the door open, they didn't notice anything unusual at first. You know, a dirty sock, a wet towel, an old tennis shoe—and then a bag with money spilling out! It looked like the bag they had used for the money from the game played at school the night before. And beyond that—little drops of blood!

"Then they saw the most horrible thing they had ever seen in their lives. It was Gail Reynolds there on the floor with a man bending over her. They couldn't see who he was because his back was turned toward the door. The students froze. They could only guess what had happened. She must have come in while he was stealing the money, and he must have decided to silence her forever. In one hand, he held a knife, and in the other hand, he held Gail Reynolds's tongue.

"When he heard them at the door, he started to turn. The students found they could move again, and they ran to the office as fast as they could. By the time they told what had happened and help arrived, Gail Reynolds was dead. The money was gone; the man was gone. But there, scrawled across the lockers in blood was the message, *'I'll get every one of you!'*

"The police never caught the man. They think he's someone who works at school, and they think he acts perfectly normal most of the time. But there's something about this time of year that sets him off. In his twisted mind, he thinks any student out of class after the final bell is one that can identify him. So every year, he comes back, and every year something terrible happens to another student at this school."

Cindy stopped speaking and looked at Carol. Carol shook her head.

"You don't really expect me to believe that, do you?" asked Carol.

"You can look it up in the library," said Betty. "It was in all the papers."

Carol made a mental note to do just that right after school.

"That still doesn't explain why you nearly splattered me running out of the locker room yesterday," she said.

"Well, there is a little more to the story," said Cindy. "See, when the killer comes back, the ghost of little Gail Reynolds comes back, too. She can't talk, but she wants to warn other students, so she takes her tongue in her hands and bangs on the lockers to warn that the killer is nearby stalking his next victim. That was the sound you heard in the locker room. That's why we told you to run and why we didn't wait."

"That's some story," said Carol.

Before she could say more, the tardy bell rang, and they all hurried off to class.

After school that day, Carol went straight to the library. She found the papers with the stories like Betty said, but there was nothing in them about the ghost of Gail Reynolds.

"They just made that part up to scare me because I'm new in school," thought Carol.

Just to be on the safe side, she vowed she wouldn't be caught alone in that building after the final bell. For a while, she kept her promise.

She decided the best way to get all that morbid stuff out of her mind was to get involved in school activities. So she volunteered to be on the decorating committee for the school dance.

The committee worked hard, and on the day of the dance, they stayed after school to put the finishing touches on the decorations. Carol went to the back to work on a special flower arrangement she was making for the faculty table. She was so absorbed in her work that a few minutes passed before she noticed she wasn't hearing the voices of her friends anymore. She looked up and realized she was alone. They had forgotten she was there, and they had gone. Once more, she was by herself in the building after the final bell.

She grabbed her purse and ran to the front door. As she pushed it open and stepped out into the chilly afternoon air, she remembered—not again!— she'd left her jacket in the locker room. There was no question about what would happen when she got home this time. After all her hard work for the dance, her mother would ground her and not let her go. There was nothing to do but go get the jacket.

She went slowly down the hall. This time, she hoped and prayed Cindy and Betty would come running out, but they didn't.

She listened at the door, and there was not a sound. It took all her courage to push the door open and look inside. She could see her jacket on the bench exactly where she left it. She took a deep breath, ran to the bench, grabbed the jacket, and dashed back toward the door. She was almost there when she heard it—a faint banging coming from behind the rows of lockers.

"Oh, God," she prayed, "please let it be a breeze banging a locker door somebody left open."

But she knew it wasn't.

The banging was getting louder now, and she could hear footsteps moving toward her behind the lockers. She ran out the door, but her foot caught in the dangling sleeve of her jacket, and she went sprawling in the hallway.

She could hear the footsteps crossing the locker room to the door now. She rolled and scooted and got to her feet. She glanced around just in time to see a shadowy figure dart back in a doorway. She headed for the front door, and she heard the footsteps start again. She was afraid to look back, afraid she might fall again. She hurried out the door and ran down the street. The footsteps kept coming behind her.

"I've got to get home," she thought. "Mom and Dad will be there. They'll know what to do."

She reached her house and fumbled for the key. She opened the door, darted through, and closed it behind her. She sagged against it to catch her breath.

"I'll calm down," she thought, "and then I'll call Mom and Dad."

As her heart got quiet, she noticed that the house was quiet, too. She saw a note on the hall table. She snatched it and read.

"Carol—We've gone to do some errands. Be back soon. Love, Mom and Dad."

"Oh, no!" she said. "Oh, no. I'm alone in this house and there's a killer outside. I—but wait. He doesn't know I'm alone. I mustn't panic. I'll be real quiet and maybe he'll go away."

Her thoughts were interrupted by a loud scra-a-a-atch.

"Oh, no," she thought. "Dad didn't put up the storm windows. That man is cutting the screen. He's going to get inside. I've got to hide, but where? Wait. I know. I'll go up to my room. I'll hide until I hear Mom and Dad. Then I'll scream, and they'll know something is wrong. They'll come up and help me."

In spite of her plan, she stood paralyzed with fear.

SCRATCH! The sound came again.

Carol bolted up the stairs to her room. She looked around for a place to hide. There was the closet, but he'd be sure to find her there. She had to do something fast. She could hear him inside now, banging around downstairs.

There was only one hiding place she could think of. She got down, rolled back under her bed as far as she could, and lay there hardly breathing.

She could hear footsteps starting up the stairs, coming closer and closer. Then she heard the most beautiful sound she had ever heard in her life—it was the sound of a second set of footsteps. It had to be Mom and Dad. They must have frightened him away.

The door opened, and the footsteps slowly crossed the room. Carol was so relieved! She rolled out from under the bed and looked up—right into the face of the killer. Beyond him she saw the reason for the second set of footsteps, for behind him stood the ghost of little Gail Reynolds, holding her tongue in her hands.

Carol heard the screaming start. It filled the room, and it filled the house, and it went on and on and on! She knew the screams were coming from her, but she couldn't stop them.

She was aware of other things going on around her. She heard the front door open and close and voices calling to her. She heard footsteps running up the stairs. She saw the ghost of Gail Reynolds disappear. She saw the killer turn and nearly knock her parents down as he plunged down the stairs and escaped one more time.

And then the screaming stopped. Her parents rushed to her.

"What happened?" they asked. "Carol, please tell us what happened!"

But Carol didn't tell them. Carol never told anybody what happened. Carol Hansen never spoke again.

Dusty

Dusty stood outside the school and looked at the sign on the building that said "Safe Place." He knew what that meant. It meant that if a kid was in trouble or had run away from home, he could come here for help and protection. Dusty knew about missing kids and safe places. Dusty was a runaway.

He just couldn't stand it at home anymore. His parents were always telling him to try to fit in, but they wouldn't even let him have a nickname. He wanted to be called Dusty, but they insisted on calling him Orion. Who ever heard of a kid named Orion? Who could fit in with a name like that? Beside, Dusty suited him.

For as long as he could remember, he had loved dirt and dust, but his mom never wanted him to get his clothes dirty.

Dusty had a talent, too, but his parents never let him practice it. Maybe someone here at school could help him practice.

School would be a great place to hide. It was warm and dry, and they had TV, a cafeteria, restrooms, books to read, and couches to sleep on in the lounge. Best of all, they had lots of dusty rooms to play in.

Dusty was wondering about the best way to get inside. Just then a group of students came up the walk, talking and laughing. When they went through the front door, Dusty followed them unnoticed.

He leaned against the wall, watching all the students hurrying to class. Nobody paid any attention to him.

From his position by the wall, he could see directly into a classroom. Mrs. Benson's name was over the door. He could see her inside writing words on the chalkboard. Just off the classroom, a door stood open, revealing a storage room filled with boxes of dusty books. This was Dusty's kind of place.

As the students entered the classroom, Dusty slipped in among them and ducked into the storage room. He had a good view of the room through the open door. He crouched behind the boxes and looked at each student.

A little blond boy in the second row caught his attention. Mrs. Benson called him Joey. He didn't seem to know many answers. When Mrs. Benson turned her back, Joey made funny faces. The class laughed, and Mrs. Benson turned unexpectedly and caught him. She gave Joey a stern warning and turned back to the board.

Dusty watched as Joey took his spelling book and placed it carefully near the edge of his desk. Little by little, he inched it along. Just as Mrs. Benson was trying to make an important point, Joey gave the book a quick shove. It hit the floor with a bang. The class laughed again.

Dusty thought it was funny, too. He liked Joey. Maybe Joey would help him practice his talent.

Mrs. Benson called the class to order.

"Joey," she warned, "I've had it with you. If you disturb this class one more time today, I'm going to make you sit in the storage room by yourself until lunch. Do you understand, young man?"

"Yes, Mrs. Benson," Joey said sweetly.

Mrs. Benson went on with the lesson. Dusty watched. Joey slowly and quietly tore a small piece of paper from his notebook. He chewed the paper into a small, juicy wad, took it out, and rolled it between his finger and thumb. Then he flipped it against the side of Mary Wilson's face. Mary shrieked. Mrs. Benson whirled around just in time to tell what had happened.

"Come with me to the storage room, Joey," she ordered.

Dusty stayed quiet. This was too good to be true. Mrs. Benson plunked Joey in a chair.

"You stay here until I come for you," she instructed.

She went back to class, and Joey remained seated.

Dusty got ready. He didn't want to scare Joey and cause him to cry out. He stood up and moved silently behind the chair. He drew himself up to his full height and pushed the hair back from his forehead. From the third eye in the middle of his forehead, he projected his deadly ray. The blond-haired Joey disintegrated into a pile of dust on the floor.

Outside Mrs. Benson was lining up the students to go to lunch. Dusty scurried back behind the boxes.

"You can come out now, Joey," called Mrs. Benson.

She waited for an answer, but when none came, she opened the door. She was totally bewildered. How in the world could he have gotten out without her seeing him?

She stepped inside, and the toe of her shoe stirred the pile of dust on the floor. She sneezed violently.

The students laughed, and Dusty smothered a giggle.

"Come, children," she ordered. "I'll have to report to the office that Joey has cut. Maybe I can get the custodian to do something about all that dust in the storage room."

She led the line of children down the hall while Dusty watched from his hiding place. Then he lay back in the dust and smiled. He had every reason to be happy. He had a unique talent, and he had found himself a safe place.

Stones

I wouldn't live by that old cemetery for anything in the world," Jerry told his new friend Paul.

Paul had just moved into the house by the cemetery, and he liked the place. From his bedroom window upstairs, he could look out over the graveyard. If the moonlight was just right, he could see those old gravestones moving and flowing and changing shape.

Paul was especially fascinated by a stone statue of an old man over one of the graves. Last night as he watched, he was sure he had seen the old man turn and look at him. His angry eyes had frightened Paul so much that he had jumped in bed and pulled the covers over his face. He had put the whole thing out of his mind until Jerry mentioned the cemetery.

"Who is the old man in that statue?" asked Paul.

"Oh, that's crazy old Mr. Goltz," said Jerry. "He used to go around saying evil spirits lived in the stones and they'd get anyone who disturbed them. One night, a boy took a short cut through there. They found him dead the next morning under a pile of stones."

71

"What happened?" asked Paul.

"People thought Mr. Goltz killed him, but he swore he was innocent. He said two local boys could account for his movements that night because they passed his car broken down way out on a county road. They had taken a friend's car for a ride without permission, so they wouldn't admit they'd seen him. They knew they'd be in trouble for being up there. They never thought the old man would get hung, but he was dead by the time they confessed."

"Why did they put that stone statue over his grave?" Paul wanted to know.

"I guess everybody felt guilty. Or maybe they were afraid. When he died, he said he'd some back to show that he was innocent," said Jerry.

"His eyes look angry," Paul said. "How did he say he would prove he was innocent?"

"Well," explained Jerry, "since those boys wouldn't vouch for his movements when he was alive, he said his spirit would live among the stones in that cemetery until some boy saw him and refused to admit it. Then he'd turn the boy to stone, and everybody would know he spoke the truth. Most people think he lives in that statue, but nobody has ever seen it move I guess."

Jerry noticed that Paul had turned very pale.

"Say, you didn't see him move, did you, Paul?" joked Jerry.

"Of course not," Paul answered quickly. "Don't be silly."

The minute those words were out of his mouth, Paul wished he could take them back.

That afternoon, Paul ran home from school without glancing at the statue. He was glad when his mom told him she'd invited Jerry and his parents to dinner. Now he wouldn't have to think about the statue.

When it was time for them to leave, Paul persuaded Jerry to spend the night. The boys went to bed. The house got quiet. Paul's parents went to sleep and the boys were about to doze off when they heard a noise: *Scrape!*

"What was that?" asked Jerry, sitting up.

"I didn't hear anything," Paul lied, but he pulled the covers tighter to shut out the sound.

SCRAPE! The sound came again, closer and louder. It was the sound of stones against stones.

"Don't tell me you didn't hear that," said Jerry.

He flipped the light on and looked at Paul. Paul was huddled in the middle of his bed shaking.

"Oh, God," said Jerry. "You lied to me, Paul. You *did* see the statue move, and now it's coming for you."

"No!" cried Paul. "It can't be. Stones can't move. I'll show you."

Paul jumped out of bed and headed for the door. The scraping sounds were right outside.

"For God's sake, don't go down there," Jerry pleaded as he ran after his friend.

Paul reached the front door and stepped outside. Clouds skimmed across the sky, hiding the moon behind their smooth gray pebble shapes. Paul moved out into the darkness.

He'd gone only a few steps when he bumped into something cold and damp and hard. He could feel something angry staring at him. He started to scream, but his voice was cut off. He felt his body flowing and changing and growing stiff.

The noise woke Paul's parents, and they ran downstairs. They heard a scraping sound move away toward the old graveyard. They found Jerry by the door, babbling.

"I saw him! He moved! I saw him," he repeated.

Paul's father ran outside. He stumped his toe and went sprawling face down on the ground.

"Oww," he muttered. "Who put this big stone in front of the door?"

A chilling wind moaned through the trees, and the moon broke free. It shone on the old stone statue in the cemetery. This time, the eyes were smiling.

Cloud Cover

I first saw it as I was traveling west on the interstate early one morning. Kelly was with me, and she saw it about the same time I did.

"Look!" she said. "There's a face peeping over that cloud."

I glanced up at the cloud bank where she was pointing, and I was so startled, I nearly swerved the car onto the shoulder of the road.

I wouldn't have believed it if I hadn't seen it with my own eyes. It was a huge head with wispy hair and two half-closed eyes staring down curiously at us. The cloud covered it up to its chin, like someone waking up in bed with a quilt pulled up.

I watched the road and tried to keep the thing in view to see how long it would be before the image dissolved. Fortunately, traffic was light.

"It's looking at us," Kelly announced in a voice that was unusually solemn for her.

It surely seemed to be. From its place in the sky, it seemed to focus its eyes on our car and stare at us for a

76

second. The car coughed and sputtered as if it were going to die, and I had a hard time holding it in the road.

Fear drizzled through my body. I'd always thought cloud shapes were fun to watch, but this... this one looked so real and so menacing, it made me tremble. I was relieved when it stopped looking at us and ducked under the cloud. The car smoothed out, and I began to relax a little.

Kelly was quiet and pale all the way to school. When I pulled up to the curb, she jumped out and ran inside as if something were chasing her.

As I drove on to work, the clouds hung low. All day, the image of a heavy-lidded face in the clouds stayed in my mind.

When I got home from work that day, Kelly's schoolbus had already dropped her off. She was sitting on the steps staring at the sky as I parked the car and came up the walk.

"I saw it again," she said.

I felt those same little drops of fear trickle through me. I didn't have to ask what she was talking about.

I didn't want to communicate my fear to Kelly, so I sat down beside her and tried to reassure her.

"The imagination plays funny tricks, honey," I told her. "There's really nothing up there. We thought we saw a face in the clouds, that's all. The storm front has moved on, and those clouds we saw this morning are miles away by now."

"But there are others coming in," she said in that grave little voice. "What if there's one of those things in every cloud? What if they've drifted in from space? What will they do to us?"

I had no answer that would satisfy her. I wasn't dealing well with my own fear. "They're clouds, sweetie, just clouds. Let's think about something else…" I searched my mind for something to distract her, "…like omelettes for supper, your favorite!"

She was quiet as she helped me with dinner. I read her a happy bedtime story before she went to sleep.

The next morning, neither of us spoke of the clouds while we drove to school. We watched them, though, as they swirled and sailed fast in the strong March wind. Then, right over the school, there was a break, and the face flashed through. As quickly, it was gone. I pretended I hadn't seen it, and Kelly didn't say a thing.

When she got out, though, she stomped her foot and said, "I *hate* the clouds! I wish they'd go away and never come back!"

As I watched her run inside, I remember, I was thinking how unlike her such an outburst was.

All morning at work, I tried to think what I should do. Should I call the police? A doctor? Would a minister be able to help? If I called someone, what would I say? "A head in the clouds has seen my little girl and me, and I think it's coming closer"? They'd put me away.

At noon, I got a call from school. Kelly had gotten hysterical, and they wanted me to pick her up right away.

She was still sobbing when I got there.

"What happened?" I asked.

"I saw it through the window," she told me. "It was watching me. When I told the teacher, it just vanished in the clouds. Then it laughed this deep, rumbling laugh. The teacher said it was thunder, but it wasn't. It was that head laughing at me."

"Many children are frightened by storms," the principal said to me. "Perhaps you should take her home now. Over the weekend, she can get a good rest, and she'll be fine on Monday."

I agreed it would be a good idea to do as he suggested. Kelly seemed calmer after we got home.

All afternoon, she sat very still, a tiny withdrawn figure at the end of the couch. She only nibbled at her dinner before going to bed.

Saturday morning, it began to rain again. Kelly was restless. I thought it might cheer her up if we went across the river to the new shopping mall.

As I drove over the bridge, I heard Kelly whimper. I looked up, and there, in a break in the clouds, I saw it again. The clouds were dropping down, closer and closer, merging with the mist from the river. Then I simply couldn't see anything at all until it happened.

I try now to look back and reconstruct the scene in my mind, but I can only remember bits and pieces. One thing I am sure of: I saw the face come out of the cloud and press against the windshield. I heard the glass shatter as those teeth began crunching through. I remember hitting the brakes and hearing the squeal of tires. There was a crash against the rail, and then I felt the car falling, falling into the river below. Kelly's screams and mine were all mixed, but I can't remember anymore.

They gave up searching for Kelly long before I came out of the coma. They told me how they rescued me, but they found no trace of her. They said her body must have been washed down the river—maybe even to the ocean. But I know that's not true. I know what happened to Kelly.

I saw that face at my windshield that morning, and I saw it again today. I looked right into its eyes, and then it leered at me and grinned and licked its lips.

"Time will heal, and you'll get better," they tell me. "It's all in your mind."

They're wrong. It's not in my mind. Nobody will believe me, but I know it's real. It's out there somewhere right now—watching, hiding, waiting behind a cloud cover.

Head Hunter

The thing hid in the shadows and stared at the window. Its eyes glittered in the moonlight as it watched Jennifer Wright pull back the curtain and look outside. Then it rolled over, and it waited.

Inside, Jennifer was waiting, too, hoping to see Michael Kincade's red sports car turn the corner and come up the street. He was working late and there was no sign of him yet, but she was relieved he was coming. She didn't want to be alone tonight.

She wished she hadn't told her brother she'd take care of his house and his dog, Buggie. She didn't like this house. Her brother had animal heads mounted all over the place, and she kept dreaming that the headless bodies of all those poor animals came back looking for their heads. Every little noise made her think of her dream.

Buggie seemed restless and uneasy, too. He seemed to sense her feelings.

Maybe she wouldn't be so upset if she could just stop thinking about the accident, but she couldn't. It had happened a year ago tonight. In a way, she blamed herself.

Maybe if she had done something differently Barry Miller would still be alive.

Everything had been fine when they first met, but after they started dating, he got so jealous and possessive she had to break it off. The threats he made were frightening, especially when she started dating Michael. Then there was the dance at the club last year when Barry made such a scene they'd asked him to leave. He'd threatened to get even with her and Michael if it was the last thing he ever did. Then he'd stormed out, got in his car, and roared off down the road.

He must have been too angry to care how he was driving. The truck driver said he was in the wrong lane and he was speeding. There was no way to avoid the crash. The whole town seemed to be there by the time Michael and Jennifer arrived. They tried to keep her from looking, but she saw it. For one split second, she saw it. It was Barry Miller's head, severed, there by the side of the road. And for that split second, those eyes glittered with recognition and focused on her accusingly. It was so horrible, she could never, never forget.

The ringing of the phone startled her back to the present. Buggie perked up his ears and looked toward the window, but Jennifer didn't hear anything but the phone. She was happy to hear Michael's voice. He was on his way. He'd be there soon.

She hung up the phone and turned around. Buggie was still acting funny. He was over by the door, whimpering and scratching to get out.

"Oh, no, you don't," she said. "I don't want to chase you around in the dark. Come on. Let's fix a snack. Michael will be hungry when he gets here."

Buggie tilted his head toward the door. He didn't move. Jennifer listened, but she couldn't hear anything.

"Come on!" she said sharply. "There's nothing out there."

Buggie didn't seem to be convinced, and she wasn't so sure either.

"Come on!" she repeated.

Reluctantly, Buggie followed her to the kitchen and sat staring at the door. She made sandwiches and broke off a bite of one and tasted it. Then she broke off a piece and offered it to Buggie. He ignored it. That was strange. Buggie never turned down food.

She saw that he was listening intently to something outside. Now she heard it, too. It was a faint noise that she couldn't identity. She poured a cup of coffee to steady her nerves. She had lifted it for a sip when she heard the noise again, closer this time. The coffee sloshed in her cup, and she struggled not to spill it as she set it down on the counter.

Something was out there—probably watching her this very minute. She couldn't deny it. She thought of her dream of all those headless animals.

She tried to calm herself. Maybe it was just the wind blowing something around in the yard.

She flipped on the radio to see if a storm was coming. Loud rock music blared at her for a few minutes before she gave up and turned it off. The silence was eerie now in contrast. She hoped the thing outside had gone away, but she heard it again.

Buggie heard it, too. His hair bristled, and he ran to the door barking.

"Be quiet, Buggie," she ordered, and she heard a sound like a low muffled laugh.

She wondered if Michael could have driven up without her hearing him while the radio was on.

"Michael, is that you?" she called.

There was no answer.

"Maybe he can't hear me through the door," she thought.

She turned the lock and opened the door just a crack.

"Michael?" she called again.

She opened the door a little more and listened. Something dashed by her, and, too late, she realized it was Buggie. She grabbed for him, but he slipped through her hands and ran across the driveway.

"Buggie, come back," she called, but he was lost in the darkness.

She was as angry with herself as she was with Buggie. Now she'd have to go look for him.

Her car keys were on the table. She snatched them and ran outside. She unlocked the car door and opened it. She stood listening for a moment, holding the keys in her hand. A bush rustled behind her and she whirled around. Her keys flew out of her hand and hit the paved drive. She stooped down, felt around until she found them, and picked them up.

Something dark flashed by her, but she couldn't tell what it was or where it went.

"Buggie, is that you?" she said aloud. "This is no time to play games."

Nothing moved, so Jennifer slid under the wheel and started the car. She backed out of the driveway and slowly cruised the street looking for the dog. The shadows cast by trees along the street made it difficult to see.

Suddenly something brushed against her leg, and she swerved.

"Buggie, you fool dog," she scolded. "Don't tell me you've been in the car all this time!"

She glanced down. The moonlight filtered through the trees and through the car window, and the glitter of something on the floorboard caught her eye.

Just then a searing pain shot through her leg, and at the same time, she saw Michael's red sports car turn the corner and speed up the street. Screams gushed from her throat as she tried to shake her leg free.

She reached for the brake, but the hideous thing on the floor shoved her foot hard against the accelerator. The car shot ahead straight into the oncoming headlights.

The explosion filled the air, and blood and bones and fire and flesh spewed into the night. Flames danced with the shadows. In the firelight by the road, two eyes glittered—and Barry Miller's head rolled off into the darkness.

Streamers

S ara woke when the storm was at its worst. The wind
shrieked and rattled the windows like something evil
trying to get in. Sara sat up, frightened. She wished now
that she had waited for Ed to finish his work and come
down with her.

She had wanted this first vacation together to be
perfect, and when some of Ed's friends she hadn't even
met offered to let them use this house in the county, it was
a dream come true. She had come down a few days early
to clean the place so she could devote all her time to Ed
when he got here.

She'd been tired from driving, so she'd gone to bed
early. She didn't know how long she'd been asleep when
the storm woke her. She looked at the clock. It was two
a.m. She wished the storm would stop, but it showed no
signs of letting up. The wind sucked the drapes against the
screen. Sara got up and hurried to close the window.

She stood for a moment looking out at the storm.
Lightning lit up the yard, and Sara could see the big tree

by the driveway. Something was hanging from the branches—something that looked like party streamers.

"Oh," she thought, "some kids must have rolled the tree with toilet paper."

She would have a closer look in the morning.

As she started to turn away, the streamers waved violently in the wind, eerie fingers reaching for her. She quickly closed the drapes and jumped back in bed. She shut her eyes to blot out the image of the strange streamers, and the steady beat of the rain lulled her to sleep.

When she woke, it was morning. Sara got up and immediately crossed to the window to see what damage the storm had done. She opened the drapes and looked at the old tree.

"That's odd," she thought. "The wind must have blown the streamers away."

She meant to look for some trace of them after breakfast, but she got so involved in her work she didn't think of the old tree or the streamers until she was in bed that night.

As she turned out the light, the wind began to moan softly, and she remembered those ghostly streamers reaching for her. She pulled the covers over her head and finally fell asleep.

This time a faint scratching woke her. It was storming again. She thought at first the wind must be blowing branches against the window. Then she remembered something and sat up fully awake. It wasn't possible. There were no branches near her window. The old tree was down by the driveway.

The scratching persisted. She looked around the room, hoping to find a logical explanation, but all was quiet—except the clock which said two a.m. again.

The wind whipped around the house and tore at the shingles. Something thumped against the window. Sara jumped up, but she approached the window cautiously. She could see nothing but inky blackness. She opened the window slowly to look out. Suddenly something rushed from the darkness and blew past her. She felt a sharp scrape against her wrist, and something hit the floor with a thud.

She jumped back and looked down. Blood was oozing from her wrist. On the floor lay an old dead limb. Just then, lightning flashed and the wind gave a howl—almost gleeful—and Sara whirled around and looked at the old tree. The streamers were back on the branches.

She had never felt so angry. She felt as if that tree had sent that limb to hurt her. And there were those crazy streamers waving merrily at her again. She'd see what they were right now.

She grabbed her robe and hurried outside. The cut on her arm was stinging, but she ignored it. She headed straight for the tree.

One second she was looking at the streamers, and the next second she was lying on the ground. She glanced around to see what had happened. She had tripped on a root.

"No, that's not right," she thought. She hadn't tripped. The root had tripped her. And she had the overwhelming feeling that it had done it deliberately!

"I must be going crazy," she told herself. "Roots don't trip people on purpose."

But this one had. She stared at it, and it even looked like a foot. The wind pulled at her robe, and she looked up at the branches above her. The streamers were gone.

She stood up and touched a limb where the streamers had been. She rubbed her hand along the bark and felt a strip of something rubberlike and sticky. She jerked her hand back and ran to the house. It wasn't until she was inside that she realized that she was still holding the sticky strip in her hand.

She examined it and shuddered. It looked like a piece of old bloody skin. She flung it in the kitchen sink and ran upstairs.

She looked in the mirror and hardly recognized herself. Her arm was streaked with blood from the scratch, and her robe was muddy from the fall. She knew she couldn't sleep, but she cleaned herself up and climbed back under the covers. She realized she was trembling. It was crazy, but something was out there. Something was out there in that old tree waiting for her. She sat huddled in her bed, half expecting that at any moment the thing in the kitchen sink would come slithering under the door. Morning was a long time coming.

When it was fully light, she crept slowly down the stairs and peeked in the kitchen. The thing was still there. It looked even more withered and repulsive in the morning light. She couldn't stand the sight of it. She grabbed it, opened the door, and threw it as far as she could. The wind picked it up, whirled it around, and dropped it in the old tree.

This was too much for Sara. She raced to the phone and called Ed's office. His secretary said he'd finished his work and was on his way. He should be there by late afternoon.

Sara felt calmer. Since she hadn't slept much, she decided to take a nap so she'd be rested when Ed arrived. She went up and lay across the bed. She slept soundly.

When she woke it was dark. Rain was beating against the window, and the wind was lashing the tree limbs in all directions. The storm had come again without warning.

She hurried to the window, hoping to see Ed's car in the drive. The drive was empty—but the branches of the old tree were filled again with those ugly streamers. She was frightened. Ed should have been here by now. As she stood there watching, bolts of lightning danced around the old tree. Then it sounded like the whole world exploded. The streamers were flung among the leaves and then driven down over the branches. Sara thought the old tree had been struck, but the storm let up and the tree was still standing.

Sara realized with a start that the phone was ringing.

She could barely hear Ed's voice saying, "The bridge washed out. I can't get through 'til morning."

Sara began to cry.

"Oh, Ed," she sobbed. "You've got to come. I am so scared. Strange streamers have been appearing and disappearing on that old tree by the driveway. I know something awful is going to happen."

Ed was silent so long Sara thought the line had gone dead. Then she heard his voice again, strained and urgent.

"Sara, I don't understand what's going on, but don't go near that tree. I never told you this because it happened a long time ago and I just didn't think it was important for you to know. You see, the family we're renting the house from once had a daughter who had a crush on me. One night at a party, I had to tell her I didn't feel the same way about her. She got angry. She rushed out in a storm and took her father's car. She must have been crying or maybe she was blinded by the storm, but she drove straight into that old tree. The car exploded and threw her body into the air. They found her hanging in strips on the branches of the old tree."

Sara was so frightened now she could scarcely breathe. Her voice was barely a whisper.

"Ed, what time did it happen?"

His voice sounded faint and far away.

"I think it was about two a.m. Why?"

The line went dead before Sara could answer. She pounded the receiver with the palm of her hand. There was no response. She looked at the clock. It was one minute until two a.m.

The storm lashed out again more furious than ever. The wind became a death wail, and leafy branches struck the window. Sara heard the crashing of glass as limbs forced their way through.

She felt herself being lifted up and out, the rain pounding against her. The wind whirled her about, and some raging, invisible force thrust her down toward the tree. In the flashes of lightning, she could see the streamers reaching for her. She flung her arms about, reaching for something to hold onto, but there was nothing. She felt herself being shredded into a thousand pieces.

The storm passed. The old tree was still. And the streamers swayed gently in the darkness.

Ghostland

Jenny Martin was a rock star. She was young and beautiful and very much in love with Johnny Robbins, a young man who played in her band.

Johnny loved Jenny, too, but he didn't want to marry her. He wanted to be a star himself, and he felt that marriage would ruin both their careers.

When the subject of marriage came up, Johnny kept putting it off. Jenny didn't like that. She was used to having her own way about everything.

Once when they were discussing the future of their relationship, Jenny grew very angry.

"I'll tell you one thing," she said. "If I can't wear your wedding ring, nobody else ever will."

Johnny just laughed at her feistiness. He loved her, and he thought their relationship would go on as before.

Then the unthinkable happened. Jenny was flying to the coast to do a show when her plane crashed and she was killed.

It hurt Johnny, but he turned to his music to forget his grief. His hard work soon earned him the fame he'd always wanted.

Jenny faded from Johnny's memory, and he began to date other girls. He met a beautiful, fun-loving girl named Cathy, and they were married in an elaborate ceremony. They took a honeymoon trip across the country to promote Johnny's latest album.

Right from the first Johnny noticed Cathy had begun to change. She didn't laugh much anymore, and she was always nervous. Johnny thought she was just feeling the pressure of being a new bride or of trying to adjust to the schedule of a rock star. Then he began to find her wedding ring lying around in the strangest places. It might be on the floor, or the window sill, or a shelf in the closet. He thought he might have bought the wrong size, so he asked her why she didn't wear her wedding ring anymore.

"You'll think I'm crazy," she said, "but every time I put that ring on my finger, something cold touches my hand and tugs at the ring. I can't get any peace until I take it off."

Jenny's words flashed through Johnny's mind, but he thought, "No, that can't have anything to do with Cathy."

He thought his wife would get better, but she didn't. Johnny took her from one doctor to another, but there was no improvement. Finally, he had to put her in an institution.

She told the doctors that every night a beautiful white hand motioned to her from the darkness. A few weeks later, she went to sleep one night and never woke up.

After Cathy's death, Johnny turned again to his music. His records continued to sell and to stay at the top of the charts. Eventually, he had everything he wanted in his professional life. He began to think about his personal relationships again.

One night at a party, Johnny met a quiet, refined lady named Peggy. He took her home that night, and after that, they were together constantly. It was only a short time before they knew they were in love.

They were married in a simple ceremony and afterward invited some friends over to dinner to help them celebrate.

The guests toasted the bride and groom, and then sat down to eat. Suddenly, Peggy gasped, dropped her fork, and grabbed her hand.

"What's wrong?" someone asked. "Did you burn yourself?"

"No," Peggy answered. "Just the opposite! I felt something cold touch my hand and tug at my wedding ring."

Everybody laughed—except Johnny.

"It's not possible," he thought.

He was remembering again what Jenny had said to him: "*If I can't wear your wedding ring, nobody else ever will.*"

Johnny sat pale and shaken.

The guests could tell that something was wrong, so they left early. Johnny and Peggy went up to bed.

It must have been about midnight when Johnny woke up. He could have sworn he heard a woman humming the "Wedding March." He thought he must have been dreaming or that Peggy was talking in her sleep. He reached over to touch her—she was cold and still. Peggy Robbins had simply stopped breathing. But there on the pillow, gleaming in the moonlight, lay her golden wedding ring.

Johnny just went from one woman to another after that, but he didn't propose to any of them until he met Mary. He knew from the beginning that Mary wouldn't settle for anything less than marriage, so they set the date.

As their wedding day approached, Johnny got nervous. He decided to say nothing to Mary about the ring, but he was obsessed with the idea that somehow Jenny would destroy Mary just as surely as she had destroyed Cathy and Peggy. He knew he had to stop her.

A plan began to form in his mind. The day before the wedding, he went out and made a few purchases. That night, he made the long, lonely journey to the cemetery where Jenny Martin was buried. He took out his new shovel and his new pick. He scooped away the earth and broke open the coffin. He reached into his pocket and took out his third and final purchase.

There in a moonlit ghostland of shadow-shrouded stones, he leaned over the open grave and said these words aloud: "With this ring, I thee wed, Jenny."

And he place the golden wedding ring on the third bone of the skeleton's left hand.

Knockers

*I*t was a dark, chilly night, and the fog hung low. The sea gulls were silent in the shrouded harbor. The only sound was the creaking of the old ships.

Ezra McCoy's family was getting ready for bed in a nearby cottage. Ezra tucked in his two little girls, Amy and Wilma, and said good night to his only son, Eric.

"Couldn't we just go down and see that old ship for a few minutes, Daddy?" asked Eric.

Ezra stood looking out the window. He could only see the bulk of the ship in the fog as it lifted and swirled down again. Something about it made the strong fisherman shudder.

"Can we go, Daddy?" Eric persisted.

"No, son," Ezra answered quickly. "This is no night for God-fearing folks to be out. I want you to stay away from that ship while it's here. There's something about it I don't like."

"Aw, Daddy," said Eric. "It's just an old ship in for repairs. Brad Hawkins says it's the biggest one he's ever seen. I want to see it."

"Me, too," echoed Amy.

"Please, Daddy," said Wilma. "It may be gone by morning."

"I hope to God it is," said Ezra. "I don't want to hear another word about it. A storm's brewing, anyway, and I don't want you out. Now hush and go to sleep."

The children lay silent, listening to their father's footsteps crossing the room and going through the little hall. They were puzzled by the harshness in his tone.

"Wonder what Daddy doesn't like about the ship?" asked Wilma timidly.

"I don't know," said Amy. "What do you think, Eric?"

"I think I'm going down and see for myself," said Eric decisively.

"Wait for us," said Wilma.

The children threw back the covers and pulled on their clothes. A few minutes later, they climbed through the window and headed down the deserted beach toward the old ship.

Inside the cottage Ezra looked at his wife, Ramona.

"I'm glad my family's safe inside tonight," he said. "That's an evil ship out there in the harbor. Sailors aren't allowed to get off and come ashore. Captain is afraid they won't come back."

"Why?" asked Ramona softly so she wouldn't wake the children.

"My father told me about that ship. It was once used for hauling slaves," explained Ezra. "Many were horribly mistreated and died. Sailors say they haunt the ship."

"Why did the sailors sign on then?" asked Ramona.

"I guess they didn't know the story," said Ezra. "They remodeled the ship. Even gave it a new name. But they didn't get rid of the evil."

The two lay listening to the rising wind and an occasional voice drifting up from the dock and finally drifted off to sleep.

On the beach, the children crept closer to the ship. The fog had thinned, and the ship loomed above them like a giant sea monster.

The rising wind began to screech and swirl the sand. Stinging rain pelted the children.

"Quick," Eric said to his sisters, "let's get back to the house."

The children turned and ran as fast as they could go. Eric was the first to reach the bedroom window. It wasn't open like they left it. The wind must have jarred it down. It was stuck fast, and Eric couldn't budge it.

The storm got worse.

"I'm scared," wailed Wilma. "I want to go inside."

"Knock on the door," said Amy. "Mommy and Daddy will let us in."

The storm raged about them, and they pounded on the doors and windows. The wind and rain drowned out the sounds of the three little knockers, and Ezra and Ramona slept peacefully.

"Let's get to the little supply boat down by the dock," said Eric.

They fought against the wind until they reached the small boat, and they climbed behind a box for shelter. The storm let up a little, and suddenly the children felt the boat moving. Men were talking, and the children stayed quiet, afraid they would get into trouble if they were discovered.

The boat stopped. They crawled inside a crate and felt it lifted. The next thing they knew, they were on the deck of the sinister old ship.

"We'll sneak out and hide until daybreak," whispered Eric. "Then we'll figure out a way to get back to the shore."

The two girls followed silently as Eric led them along the deck, down a ladder, and through a dark passageway. They came to an empty room.

"Look," said Amy. "There are bars on the window."

"Wonder what they used this room for?" asked Wilma.

"I don't know," said Eric. "But let's try to get some sleep so we can sneak out tomorrow."

The three children huddled together in the vacant room where slaves had huddled many years before. While they slept the storm blew itself out, and the ship weighed anchor and sailed out to sea.

Sailors who came on deck to take the morning watch saw the open hatch.

"Who opened this?" the first sailor wanted to know.

"Not me!" said the second. "I wouldn't go near that hole. Close it fast!"

The children woke in the morning, and all they could see from the little barred window was water. They screamed and beat on the walls, but nobody answered the little knockers.

On deck, the sailors hurried past the closed hatch.

"The spirits are restless this trip," they muttered.

Finally the sounds ceased.

Now, they say that when a storm is brewing, knocks sound at the little cottage by the ocean. The grief-stricken parents rush to answer, hoping for a sign of their lost children. They stare at the ocean that took the most precious things in their lives, but it gives back nothing. The knocking goes on, but the beach is deserted, except for seaweed and driftwood.

Tree Talk

Cornelia stood near the street light every morning and looked at the three wooden figures in the museum window—figures so human they seemed to be trying to speak.

The two wooden women sat side by side with their backs to the window. The man sat across the table facing them and the street. At first, the man seemed to be trying to talk to the women, but lately, Cornelia thought, he seemed to be trying to talk to her.

She found herself avoiding that side of the street. She began walking down the other side and standing near the old tree stump until the school bus came.

By the streetlight one morning she noticed some carving low on the old dead trunk. She leaned over for a closer look and saw that it was a whole sentence.

She could just make out the words: "To grow is to reach out as well as up."

Cornelia wondered who carved it and what the carver had meant by those words.

For several mornings, she stared at the huge old tree stump. Now she had the feeling that *it* was trying to tell her something, too. She shivered and backed away.

The next morning, she walked on the museum side of the street again. She tried to ignore the three figures in the window, but the urge to look was irresistible. The man's wooden eyes bore into hers, willing her to come closer. As she pressed her face against the glass, she saw that the wooden figures were made of oak—the same wood as the old tree stump! She wondered why she hadn't noticed before. All at once she realized that the man had somehow pointed it out to her.

Cornelia turned and ran to the bus stop, relieved that the bus pulled up just then and she could board.

All day she thought about the figures and the lonely old tree stump. That night, she saw them in her dreams. In the morning, she seriously considered pretending to be sick and staying home from school, though she knew that was out of the question. Besides, she couldn't stay home every day. Sooner or later, she'd have to go back to the bus stop. It might as well be today.

She waited as long as she dared and ran by the stump and the museum window without stopping to glance either way. The bus was right on time. She was grateful that she didn't have to wait.

She was jittery all day at school and made so many mistakes she was sure she'd never finish her work on time. She dropped her books in the hall and almost missed her bus.

When it stopped at the corner to let her off, she was startled to see the museum was open. Without thinking, she looked at the figures. The man's eyes seemed to plead with her to come inside. She decided on impulse that maybe she should.

Inside the museum the air seemed heavy and cold. Cornelia spotted a young man behind a desk. As she approached, he stared at her from the dimness. She couldn't see his face very well, but she could tell he was dressed in a costume from the same period as the carved statues.

"Could you tell me about the figures in the window?" she asked.

"It's a gruesome story," he warned her. "You might not want to hear it."

"Oh, I'm very curious," Cornelia told him. "Please go ahead."

"Well," he began, "the figures were made from the old tree across the street when it was cut down. They are carved in the likeness of three people who died in that tree many, many years ago."

Cornelia turned a little pale as she listened to the young man.

"You see," he continued, "the young man was in love with the first young lady you see sitting there. She was poor, and the young man's rich family pressured him into marrying the other girl that you see beside the first. The second girl was rich, and such a marriage would elevate the young man's family even more in society."

"Why didn't the young man just run away with the girl he really loved?" asked Cornelia.

"Perhaps he lacked the courage to defy his family. In any case, he met his true love by that very old oak tree to tell her that he was marrying another," answered the young man.

"What happened then?" Cornelia wanted to know.

"Nothing happened at first. The poor girl was not seen until the morning of the wedding. They found her hanging from the big limb of the old oak," said the young man. "The story goes that the young man sat all afternoon under the tree. He mumbled something about social climbers to a couple of men who passed, and he carved the words in the tree trunk that he was not brave enough to say to his family."

"Yes," said Cornelia. "I saw that. It said, 'To grow is to reach out as well as up.'"

"Yes," said the young man. "That's what he carved. Well, the wedding took place in the late afternoon. The guests hurried from the church to the bride's home under threatening skies. As the bride and groom rode in their carriage, the storm broke. They were passing under the old oak tree when lightning struck the very branch where the poor girl had been hanging. The branch crashed into the buggy and both bride and groom were killed."

"Why did they cut down the tree?" inquired Cornelia.

"You know how people are," explained the young man. "They began to imagine they heard voices in the tree, and they said they were the voices of the unfortunate lovers. When the tree was cut a young artist took the wood and carved the figures, which he donated to the museum. When he went on his way, the figures lay covered in dust down in the basement for years. The old man who is curator now found them and put them on display."

"They don't seem to be very happy about it," observed Cornelia.

"They aren't," agreed the young man. "It's painful for them to have their grief exposed to the world. Perhaps it is the young man's fate to be bound to the two women he destroyed. Perhaps they would all like to be left alone to rest in peace."

Just then a door opened behind Cornelia, and she turned to see the old curator coming toward her.

"How can I help you, miss?" he asked.

"I was just talking to the young man behind the desk here about the carved figures in the window," she replied.

"What young man?" he asked her.

She turned and looked. He was gone. She felt her knees give away, and the old man helped her to a chair and brought her water.

"Now if you feel up to it, tell me what he said," the old man urged.

She repeated the story and the old man shook his head.

"That's incredible," he told her. "You see, my grandfather was the young artist who carved those figures years and years ago. When I came here and took over the museum, I found them in the basement and put them in the window. My grandfather told me that story when I was a little boy. As far as I know, people around here now don't know what happened."

Cornelia and the old curator moved to the window. The wooden figures sat in their places unchanged. Cornelia ran her fingers along the smooth wood of the young man's hand and started to go. She felt a little jab and looked down. There was a tiny splinter in her finger. She looked at the wooden statue. The young man's eyes were wet with tears.

All That Glitters

*S*ome people said that old Joe Warren had been born with a silver spoon in his mouth. Others said that if he was, he probably threw it down and demanded a gold one.

Joe Warren had a number of "golden years" before he reached old age. What he thought of every year in his life was gold.

He life could be divided into four periods.

There were the first, glittering years, when, as a young man from a family with money, he went off to law school. After he graduated, he was more concerned with helping himself to hefty retainer fees than with helping clients, though, in the process, all parties usually came out winners.

The second period came when he discovered there was a certain golden-haired beauty with more gold in her family than Fort Knox had in its vault. He wasted no time in staking his claim there. At first, she was flattered that he called her Goldie, but after several years and several children, the title lost its luster.

Some said Goldie died of a broken heart because she was starved for love. Others suspected cancer since she just sort of withered away to nothing. A few wondered if Joe Warren had helped his wife cross over, because when she died, Mr. Warren became a very wealthy man.

Within a year, the glittering Joe had dazzled another flaxen-haired beauty whose pockets and vaults were also lined with gold. In less than two years, she, too, was dead from a wasting disease. Joe Warren was richer than ever.

For a while he seemed satisfied to assess his assets. He was so preoccupied with his gold that his children left home as soon as they were old enough. Joe Warren really didn't care very much. If anything, he was glad to have them working on their own.

"You don't need anyone," his daughter once told him. "All you need is your precious gold."

But as she watched her father growing older and withdrawing more and more into himself, she knew she was wrong. He did need someone.

She urged him to go out and meet people, and finally, to get her off his back, he agreed.

He met woman after woman, but none pleased him. One was too old, one was too young. One was too witty and got all the attention. One had no sense of humor, he said, but in truth, she got tired of explaining jokes to him and left. He found something wrong with each one because to him they had one fault in common—they didn't have enough money.

He'd about given up when some friends invited him over for a game of bridge. His partner was a tall, blond widow. She had consoled herself after her husband's death by having various parts of her anatomy nipped and tucked and uplifted and stretched. She reeked of money, and for Joe Warren, it was love at first sniff.

Old Warren moved fast. Mary Candry was elated that she had finally met a man with his own money—a man who would love her for herself. They skipped the engagement and went right to the marriage. Joe entered the fourth and final phase of his life without recognizing that he had met his match.

It didn't take Mary long to realize that dear Joe was not the pot of gold at the end of her rainbow. He was more like a chamber pot. The way he treated her stank, and he bored her to distraction. The man was all spit and shine and no substance. She began to wonder how she could extract herself from this sticky situation with the least possible expense.

Perhaps old Joe Warren read her thoughts. His attitude toward her began to change. He grew concerned that she looked tired, and he began bringing her a cup of hot herbal tea each night to help her sleep. Soon Mary began to waste away like the other two who had had the misfortune to bear Joe Warren's name.

Mary noticed he monitored her calls. She had dialed her doctor one night when old Warren caught her. He stood looking down at her, and he knew that she knew. He promised to take her to the doctor the next morning, but that night, he made the tea stronger than usual.

Mary knew too late what he had done.

"You'll pay for this," she whispered. "People will see death in your face after I die, for you have killed me."

Old Warren buried his wife and went home alone, with only his gold and his memory of those last words for company. Many had come to the funeral out of respect for

Mary, but none came to the old house to offer Joe Warren comfort. People had begun to wonder about his outliving three rich wives who had died in similar ways.

Old Warren became something of a recluse. Stories circulated that three golden globes of light danced around his house at night. People began to avoid the area. No one ever saw him outside. He had his groceries delivered and left the money in an envelope on a table in the hall.

One day in late fall, the fire department answered a call. Neighbors had spotted a fire in the old Warren house. Sirens wailed, and people in town dropped what they were doing and followed the fire trucks. They stood watching the flames flare out and shoot up, and they wondered if the old man was still inside.

Just then, the door opened and old Joe Warren stumbled out. One fireman dropped his hose, and the people standing nearby gasped and screamed and stepped back. No wonder the old man had stopped coming outside; he was too frightening.

He stared at the crowd for a moment from eyes sunk far back in their sockets. They stared back, transfixed.

The skin on the old man's face was stretched tight against his bones, and his hair was entirely gone. His scalp and the skin of his face had such a yellow cast that they looked like gold. He stood there, his wasted body topped by a living, golden skull.

Nobody could move. Nobody could turn away. Suddenly, from out of the inferno, three red-gold balls of fire swirled down on old Joe Warren. His clothes flashed into flames, and he fell to the ground rolling and screaming. The firemen tried to approach, but the heat was of such unnatural intensity that it drove them back.

When the flames died, the air was filled with sulfur-scented smoke. The body on the ground was charred and the skull was a melted glob of gold gleaming in the sun.

Bag Lady

With a gloved hand, Lola Meece pulled the weed from among the daffodils and stacked it neatly with the others that lay beside her. She adjusted her wide-brimmed hat to protect her delicate skin from the mid-morning sun. As she brushed back a strand of long red hair, a movement on the sidewalk beyond the hedge caught her attention. She stood up and saw that hideous woman staring at her again.

She'd first seen the woman Saturday when she'd taken Fifi for a walk in the park. Lola had dragged poor Fifi away as soon as she noticed the old woman watching them. It had been bad enough to see such a shabby and disreputable woman walking around in a public park frequented by respectable people, but it shocked Lola to see this same old bag lady in front of her own house, peering at her over the hedge.

"A disgrace to the neighborhood," Lola muttered to herself. "Al and I contribute to agencies every year to handle these problems. I won't stand for this kind of thing on my street!"

Lola knew the woman must be sent on her way at once, but certainly *she* wanted no personal contact with the miserable creature. She hurried inside to find one of the servants.

As her housekeeper confronted the bag lady, Lola Meece watched from her window. The woman was bent and thin, but not the least bit intimidated. She stared at the window where Lola was watching, and then she deliberately stepped onto the lawn, crossed to the flower bed, and broke off a daffodil.

That was really too much! Lola flew out the door in a fury.

"Get out at once!" Lola ordered, running toward the old woman and the servant. "How dare you trespass on my property?"

The woman looked at her calmly.

"I only wanted a flower," she said. "Where I come from, flowers are for everybody."

"Then go back to where you came from," Lola demanded. "You don't belong here."

The old lady walked wordlessly to the edge of the yard before she stopped and looked back.

"It's strange," she said quietly, "but life takes some of us through many twists and turns before it shows us where we belong. It's not over for either one of us yet."

Lola was shaking as she watched the old woman walk slowly down the street. She wasn't sure if she shook from anger or from fear, because the old woman's words sent chills prickling through her body.

She realized her housekeeper was urging her to go inside to prepare for her luncheon, so she went along, trying to put the incident out of her mind.

Two hours later, surrounded by friends at tables set up on the lush green lawn by the lake, Lola shared the unpleasant experience. They all agreed that the state of the homeless was indeed unfortunate, but they all knew that people must take control of their lives. Surely these street people had lost control through some fault of their own.

Lola felt better when her guests had gone. She climbed down the bank and sat feeding the swans and gazing at her own reflection in the water. The daffodils along the bank dazzled her with their brightness.

Today they reminded her of Al's teasing. Al liked to tease her when he was home between his endless business trips. He called her his little daffodil, because daffodils are a kind of narcissus. He said he only wanted her to be beautiful for him and not to worry her pretty head about business. He'd even bought her a book of Greek mythology with the legend of Narcissus in it.

She loved the story of the beautiful youth who refused the love of the nymph Echo and whom Aphrodite punished by making him fall in love with his own image. She understood how he pined away, gazing at this reflection in a clear pool, and she rejoiced that the gods took pity and changed Narcissus into a beautiful flower bending its head over the water.

Lola felt confident that she would always be beautiful for Al and that she could always count on him to take care of her. Tonight he'd be home, and they'd laugh about the presumptuous bag lady.

As she moved back from the water, for just a second, the surface rippled, and she thought she saw the face of the old bag lady instead of her own. She blinked, and it was gone.

She had the uneasy feeling that someone else was in the room as she dressed for dinner, and she stole a number of quick, sidelong glances at the several mirrors. She saw only her elegant self.

At eight o'clock, Lola had dinner alone. Al had been late before. There was probably some delay at the airport. At nine, she was anxious. At ten, she snatched up the phone on the first ring.

The days that followed were a blur. The news of the plane crash had barely sunk in when the phone rang again and again, with reporters and sympathizers and people simply eager for morbid details. Then there was the funeral and that devastating meeting with the lawyers.

It couldn't be true. This couldn't be happening to her. She had always been in control, hadn't she? Al couldn't be dead. He couldn't have left her destitute. The lawyer said Al had gambling debts and that she must leave the house in thirty days so it could be sold. There had to be some dreadful mistake.

The servants left because she could no longer pay them. She wandered around the house dazed, knowing she had to make plans and take charge yet unable to do so. Friends who used to flock to the luncheons and grand parties never called now or came around. Calls Lola placed were not returned.

Twice she saw the old bag lady walk by and pick daffodils, but she no longer cared.

Each morning, Lola gazed in the mirror and saw a stranger looking back. Each time, she saw more wrinkles crisscrossing her face and more pounds melting away from her body. By the end of a month, she knew something was terribly wrong, but she didn't know what to do about it.

Then the lawyer called again, telling her she must be out of the house by the afternoon. She had no place to go, but that didn't seem to bother anybody but her.

As she was packing a few things in her bag, she noticed one of Al's shirts on the closet floor. She picked it up and reached in the pocket from habit, as if life were the same as it had always been. She withdrew a piece of paper and was surprised to see that it was a lottery ticket. She hadn't known Al played the lottery.

Suddenly she was angry. How could Al have squandered their money on things like this? She thrust it into her pocket along with her gardening gloves. The anger left her weak and trembling.

She closed the door behind her for the last time. Her legs wobbled as she crossed the lawn. The grass had grown high beside the flower bed, and she sank down in it to rest for a moment.

She looked at the beautiful daffodils, choked now by weeds and beginning to fade. She would pull just a few of those ugly weeds, and then she'd find someone to help her plan what to do. They had agencies for things like that.

She took out her gloves to protect her hands. She didn't notice the lottery ticket flutter from her pocket; she was staring at her hands. She saw that she was pulling her gloves over bones covered with no more than loose skin.

She groaned once, and then again. She tried to scream, but the sound stuck in her throat. Nothing came out but the groans. She looked at her arms and legs, and there was nothing to them. She was a skeleton draped with folds of skin, a literal bag of bones.

Another sound merged with Lola's groans. The wind moaned and bent the daffodils and flapped the empty hide. It picked up the winning lottery ticket and carried it over the hedge.

The old bag lady coming along the street heard the groaning and started to investigate, but the wind dropped something at her feet. She hesitated. That woman would just get angry again if she caught her on her property. The bag lady picked up the ticket and hurried away to check the numbers.

Beyond the hedge, life twisted and turned, and the withered daffodils bowed low along the water.

Justice

*D*aryl Ralston and John Hampton waved their hands. Mrs. Fuller ignored them. They always had an answer. Often it was not the one she wanted the class to hear.

She looked over the faces suddenly studying the floor or looking for something in their notebooks.

"Can anyone define justice for me?" she repeated to the class.

Daryl and John continued to wave frantically. Mrs. Fuller looked hopefully around for someone else to respond. No one did. She sighed.

"All right, Daryl," she said. "Tell the class the meaning of justice."

"Justice is the opposite of injustice," said Daryl, looking around for the laughter that was sure to follow.

It did.

"Quiet, class," ordered Mrs. Fuller. "I am afraid that doesn't tell us much, Daryl. Can you be more specific?"

Mrs. Fuller had a special reason for discussing justice today. As she pulled into the school parking lot, she had seen Daryl and John and some of their friends holding a bird's nest. The baby birds were dead on the ground. With solemn eyes, they swore to her they had not done it, but she knew better. She had seen them laughing.

They laughed at her sometimes, too, when they thought she wasn't aware of it. She knew. They left feathers on her desk, and she heard them call her the Bird Lady or Old Crow behind her back, but she didn't care. She loved the little helpless creatures.

She was aware suddenly that she had drifted off. When she had these spells, the students said she'd "tripped south for the winter." She'd done it again. She forced herself back to the classroom. The class was watching her closely.

"Well, Daryl, I'm waiting for an answer," she said.

"I just told you," said Daryl. "Justice means that somebody gets what's coming to him."

"Yeah," John put in. "Like somebody kills someone and then has to die for it."

"Yeah," agreed Daryl. "Like that."

The two boys exchanged the look that said it was time to bait Mrs. Fuller.

"For instance," continued John, "take those itty bitty birds that we found dead in the parking lot. Whoever killed them ought to die a painful death. I don't ever want to see anything like that again. If those guys got what was coming to them, now *that* would be justice."

The mock-serious tone brought giggles from different sections of the room. Only a few felt sorry about this daily routine that the two boys put Mrs. Fuller through.

They waited to see what her response would be today. She was quiet so long, they had begun to think she had "tripped south" again.

"Perhaps you're right," she finally said. "We've talked in this class about how you feel when, as teenagers, you experience unpleasant things, unjust things, because of your age or sex or color. Sometimes you have no more control over the injustice of a situation than those innocent little birds did yesterday. But it seems that learning to value all life is a lesson some of you have not learned. Maybe fate will teach you what I have not been able to."

She smiled oddly at the class as the bell rung.

The class filed out silently for the first time. Mrs. Fuller had never said anything like that before. They stood by their lockers and watched as she walked down the hall and stopped by the front door.

Daryl and John were a little uneasy. This was not the reaction they had hoped for. They didn't feel quite so much in charge as they usually did.

"Come on," said Daryl. "Let's go find some more birds' nests."

John laughed and started down the hall behind Daryl. Slowly the others followed. Mrs. Fuller stood by the door smiling that odd smile, and the students filed past her on their way home.

John and Daryl sat on the school steps out by the street wondering what had gone wrong. Mrs. Fuller didn't *seem* upset with them. She was just standing in there watching them.

"I'm getting out of here," John said at last. "I think the old bat is off her rocker."

As John stood up, a feather floated down and brushed his face. Startled, he looked over at Daryl.

Daryl was looking up.

There was a loud swishing sound as two huge birds swooped down on the boys. Sudden screams filled the air, and students walking down the street stopped in their tracks and turned around. They stood frozen in disbelief. Two gigantic birds were covering John and Daryl, clawing their faces and pecking at their eyes.

The door opened and Mrs. Fuller came out. Daryl and John waved their hands frantically in the air. Mrs. Fuller smiled the odd smile and ignored them. This, she thought, was the answer she'd been waiting for.

Earthbound

M arty got out near the church and headed down the road to the old farm he loved. He couldn't remember exactly how long he'd been away. He hadn't wanted to leave in the first place, but some things couldn't be helped. He'd had no choice.

The worst thing about leaving was the way his mother had cried. He'd been the only one left to help her work the farm, but he hadn't been able after the accident. He wouldn't be coming back now except for his mother's grieving. She hadn't actually asked him to come, but he could tell by her crying she wanted him to.

His legs felt wobbly as he walked along because he wasn't used to walking. He had to go slowly, but he didn't mind. It gave him a chance to look at the farm. Most things hadn't changed, yet something was different. It gave Marty a peculiar feeling because he couldn't figure out what it was. He felt out of place, and that disturbed him.

He knew every inch of those corn fields, and he knew he'd always be bound to that land. The wind was picking up, and he could hear the corn rustle like corn fairies whispering. He remembered how his mother used to read him that story by Carl Sandburg.

In the farmhouse down the road, Marty's mother was thinking about the old days, too. She was wishing this stormy night could be like those when the family was together. Her husband would come in from the fields, and they'd sit around the fire after supper and she'd read to Marty. After her husband died, she had still had Marty, and he had been such a comfort. She dreaded stormy nights now that she was alone. This would be a bad one. The first clap of thunder had jarred Marty's picture right off the wall.

Back down the road, Marty tried to walk faster. He thought he'd be home by the time the storm broke, but he was very tired now. Every breath he took burned his lungs. His throat felt dry and dusty, and his shoes were covered with dirt.

He could see the shape of the old barn looming in the distance now. The combine would be inside. It was odd, but he hadn't thought of it since the accident.

He saw the farm house beyond and wished the black clouds wouldn't roll in so fast.

He really needed to hurry, but his body wouldn't respond like it used to.

As he passed the barn, the air felt heavy and damp and there was a strong musty odor around him. Something definitely was not right, and it worried him.

But he was almost home. He could see the light in the window, and he knew his mother would be happy to see him. He wondered if she'd think he'd changed much.

The first raindrops hit as Marty reached the yard. His energy was spent, but he forced himself to keep going. He could hardly wait to see his mother's face.

The storm began to rage around him as he climbed the steps to the porch. The wind tore at his clothes and drove him against the railing. He stumbled and grabbed the old porch swing. His weight banged it against the side of the house.

Marty's mother heard the noise, and through the window, Marty saw her move to the door to see what had happened. As the door opened, he turned toward her and gave her his biggest smile.

For a few seconds, she stood there blinking, trying to adjust to the darkness. She smelled a musty, rotten odor, and then a flash of lightning revealed the figure before her. In an instant, she saw the grinning skull and the rotting burial clothes of her dead son. She stared in disbelief as the thing from the grave reached out to her. Then Marty's mother fell forward into the skeleton's bony arms.

Dinner

Jimmy Butler decided he'd show them all! They had laughed at him for the last time. He'd heard all the names he could stand.

"Fatty! Fatty!"

"Scaredy-cat!"

"Chicken!"

"Fatso!"

He knew he was fat. He knew he was scared of almost everything. He didn't need them to tell him. He knew that someday something would probably frighten him to death. He just couldn't stop eating or being afraid all the time.

He wanted so much for them to like him! He tried to diet to be trim like they were, but he'd fail a test or do something stupid in gym, and the teasing would start again. It hurt, and eating made him feel better.

Camping trips were out of the question. He'd tried to fit in there before. When the other kids found out he was afraid of the dark, and of ghosts especially, they made his life miserable.

Jimmy had become a loner at school. He had no friends after school, either. He ate; he slept; he went to school; he came home. He longed to be one of the group. He'd do anything!

One Friday afternoon, some of the guys approached him near his locker as he was heading for the door to go home.

"Where ya going, Chicken-Boy?" they asked him.

Jimmy didn't answer.

They formed a half circle, blocking his way. They were clearly waiting for him to say something.

"Home," he mumbled.

"How'd you like to join our club?" they asked.

Jimmy trembled. Could he be hearing right? Him? In their club?

"Well, sure," he answered.

"Not so fast!" they told him. "First, you have to be initiated."

Jimmy felt the old familiar tightening in his stomach. He knew he'd never make it. It would be a trick, a big joke! He thought about the candy bars he had at home, hidden in his desk. But this was probably his last chance to be with the others. Whatever they had in mind, he'd have to try.

"What do I have to do?"

The boys looked at each other. They knew and Jimmy knew that they had him now.

"We have a little welcoming dinner planned especially for you tonight at the old Kramer Lodge," they said. "We'll drop you off at the edge of the woods, and you'll have to walk up the trail alone in the dark to meet us."

"Bu-but, the Kramer Lodge is supposed to be hau-haunted," stammered Jimmy.

"You'd miss out on joining our club because of some silly old stories?" they asked. "We don't want a coward around!"

"Coward!"

"Fat Freak!"

"Chicken!"

"OK!" said Jimmy. "I'll show you who's a coward. Pick me up before dark."

Jimmy knew he would literally die if he saw a ghost. But he had to show them. More than anything, he needed to belong.

It was dusk when the boys picked him up. He stuffed his hands in his pockets to keep them from shaking. He could feel the candy bars he had hidden in his pockets for an emergency snack. That seemed to comfort him a little.

"Maybe we'll all go to the big game in Greensville after dinner," they told him. Jimmy relaxed a little more. Maybe he should dare to hope this time; maybe he'd make it.

The boys dropped him off at the foot of the trail. Jimmy watched as the taillights disappeared around the bend.

"Get going!" he told himself. "The sooner you get started, the sooner it will all be over."

As Jimmy moved through the woods, darkness came swiftly. He heard noises all around, noises he'd never heard before. A dead branch snapped behind him. He whirled, twisting his right ankle and falling hard. The pain shot red-hot up to his knee. He struggled up and tried to put his weight on it. It still hurt, but he could stand. He was fairly certain it wasn't broken. He spotted a long stick by the trail that he could lean on.

He had to go on. The boys would be waiting. But what if they weren't? How would he get home with a sprained ankle? He might be able to walk back down the trail, but not all the way home. And what would he eat? He didn't want to spend the night in the woods. He was really frightened now. And he was getting hungry.

His hands were sweaty as he reached for one of the candy bars in his pocket. He tore it open and stuffed the whole thing in his mouth. He had promised himself he wouldn't eat until dinner, but he couldn't help it. He needed all his strength to get up to the lodge.

He sighed as he hobbled into the clearing. Just beyond was a light in the old lodge dining room. No repairs had been made since the fire that killed a dozen people had closed it down. His friends were probably waiting in the dining room. He'd half expected to see them waiting outside to taunt him, but he bet they thought he'd be too scared to come, and besides, the sprained ankle had slowed him down. They must have started without him.

He hurried as fast as he could. Now he could hear the dishes rattling and chairs being moved up to the table. He could smell the hot bread, and his mouth watered as he moved up to the window.

His heart stopped when he looked inside. This couldn't be happening. Steaming bowls of food were being passed around for the evening meal. But something was wrong. There was something missing. There were no people at this dinner.

Before he could move, the door blew open, and ghostly voices laughed and called his name.

"Come in, Jimmy. We've been waiting for you!"

"What's going on?" Jimmy managed to ask in a squeaky voice. "Where are my friends?"

"We've just enjoyed having them for dinner," cackled a voice at the table. "*You* are going to be our dessert."

"He's plump and juicy, just like I like 'em," said another. "Let's warm him up."

Invisible hands yanked him through the door, and it slammed shut behind him. Once again, the fire burned and guests feasted at the old Kramer Lodge. And Jimmy Butler was finally part of a group.

The Pumpkin People

*M*any, many years ago, there was a little village where people farmed the land and hunted deer and quail. Their lives were happy and peaceful except for one thing. Once a year, at harvest, they found themselves at the mercy of a giant race of beings. These beings had eyes that glowed like jack-o'-lanterns and skin so orange that the villagers called them the Pumpkin People.

The Pumpkin People lived deep in the earth, but at harvest time, they raided the village seeking furs and food. When they knocked on the villagers' doors, they expected these things to be waiting. If they weren't waiting, the Pumpkin People would leave and return at midnight to punish those who refused to give them what they wanted. The punishment for those who failed the Pumpkin People had always been too terrible to think about.

One year, a drought struck the land, and the crops failed. The villagers were barely able to harvest enough food for their own families. Game was scarce because the animals had died or left for lack of water. When it was time for the Pumpkin People to come, the poor villagers had little to give them. Knowing the consequences of leaving nothing, they put out what little they had.

Only one man refused to share. Peter Vingle put out nothing. He had lost his wife when his little daughter was born, and he treasured the child more than anything. She was perfect, except for a tiny birthmark—the outline of a star on her cheek. Peter thought that was beautiful, too, so he named the little girl Starlina. She was the one bright spot in his life, and he was determined he would have enough food to feed her through the winter.

"Let the Pumpkin People grow their own food," he said.

He tried to convince the foolish people to keep their food for themselves, but they looked at him with frightened eyes and begged him not to anger the Pumpkin People.

"They have warned us," said the villagers, "'Give us something you've planted, or we'll take something of yours to plant.' Please give them something. Nobody knows what will happen if you don't."

Peter Vingle heeded no warnings. He had made up his mind. He looked at the food and furs that the villagers had sacrificed, and he shook his head.

"After tonight, they'll know how silly they've been," he thought. "And they needn't come crawling to me for help."

The night they all dreaded came, and after dark, Peter heard the knocking. He did not answer. He fed Starlina her supper and tucked her in bed. Then he ate and went to bed himself, for the day had left him weary.

He heard the knocking again at midnight, but he did not get up. He buried his head between his pillows and slept on. He didn't hear the little feet patter softly to the door to answer the knock. It wasn't until morning came and he went to wake Starlina that he discovered she was gone.

He frantically sounded the alarm, and all the villagers joined in the search. They shook their heads sadly, and Peter Vingle flew into a rage when they suggested that she had been taken by the Pumpkin People.

When the day ended, there was still no sign of the little girl. They called off the search, and Peter walked home with his head bowed in grief.

As he started to open his door, he noticed a single pumpkin seed on the ground. Anger boiled through him, and he stomped the seed into the earth.

Winter came, and Peter Vingle's hair turned white to match the snow. He went into the village only when he had to.

Finally it was spring—the time of rebirth. Everything was blooming and growing. It was going to be a good year for crops.

One day, Peter stepped outside and noticed for the first time that a pumpkin vine was growing by the door, and it had one small pumpkin on it. He looked closer and fell to his knees in disbelief.

Eyes glowed from the pumpkin like jack-o'-lanterns, but he knew the features well. The star outline was perfect on the cheek.

The air grew cold, and a voice echoed from deep within the earth: "Give us something you've planted, or we'll take something of yours to plant."

The pumpkin vine flew into the air and wrapped itself around Peter Vingle's neck. All went black as he fell across the glowing eyes of the pumpkin.

Storm Walker

*A*s a child in Appalachia, I was never afraid of ghosts and goblins. I was scared of thunderstorms. When I'd be sitting in the little one-room school I attended, I could look out the window and see the awesome black clouds boiling up over the Appalachian foothills along Russell Creek. When I got caught in those storms on the way home from school, I realized I was not a good storm walker.

If the teacher saw the storm coming in time, she would dismiss school early and tell us to hurry home. I'd run a short way down Highway 80 and then cut across the fields along the old road that led to our farm.

Some days like that would bring me a little bit of luck. I'd see our neighbor Jim coming down the road from town and run to catch up with him so we could walk home together. I felt safe with Jim because he was a good storm walker.

The wind would bend the trees in the dark pine grove that we had to pass, and the lightning might hit the barbed-wire fence and run along the road close by us. It would be close enough to make me tingle, but I felt that somehow Jim would protect me.

As we walked, Jim would give me advice about storm walking.

"Don't take shelter under a single tree. The lightning might strike it. And if the wind is blowing hard, get down in a gully."

I listened to everything he said, and I thought I would remember.

At the end of my first school year, Jim became ill. The doctor said it was his heart, so Jim didn't walk much anymore. I visited him during the summer, and we sat under the shade trees in his yard while he whittled dolls for me.

Then school began, and I dreaded those walks alone. Fall and winter came and went, and the walks home were uneventful. But spring brought the thunderstorms I dreaded.

One afternoon at school, I looked out the window and saw yellowish-green clouds looming over Russell Creek Hill. It was almost time for school to be over, so the teacher let us go with instructions to hurry home as fast as we could.

She didn't need to tell me to hurry. I ran up the road and cut across the fields until I reached the old pine grove. The storm had changed its course, and it was sweeping along the path in my direction. I had already run until there were pains in my side, and I knew I would never outrun it. Lightning struck nearby, and I felt the familiar tingle. I forgot all of Jim's warnings. In my panic, I simply wanted any kind of shelter I could find, so I dashed under a tall tree and stayed huddled there while the fury of the storm grew.

I don't know how much time passed; I'm sure it wasn't long, but it seemed forever. Sheets of rain whipped in the wind. Then, for a moment, it was calm. It wasn't lightning, but the air was charged with electricity. The grove was enveloped in eerie silence. I began to tingle and I heard a roaring. I knew I should get out from under the tree, but I didn't know where to go. I had never ventured back in the dark pine grove. I looked around wildly for a place to hide, and then I saw a familiar figure walking quickly toward me through the storm.

The roar was too loud for me to hear him speak, but Jim motioned for me to follow him. I ran after him to a gully back in the grove. He gestured for me to get down, and I did. I looked back just in time to see a black, twisting cloud dip down and uproot the very tree I'd been huddled under.

I covered my head and stayed down until the roaring had died away. When I raised my head, Jim was gone and the rain had stopped.

While I was wondering where Jim had taken cover, I heard my name being called. I scrambled out of the gully and ran toward the sound. My father was coming across the field to look for me. I ran to meet him, and he carried me home. I was so tired, I fell asleep.

When I woke up, I was safe at home. Mom had saved me some supper with my favorite fried apple pies for dessert. While I ate, Mom and Dad told me how proud they were that I had known what to do when the tornado hit.

"I didn't," I confessed. "I was hiding under a tree when Jim showed me where to go."

My parents exchanged glances.

"Honey," my mom said gently, "Jim couldn't have shown you where to go. He died at noon today."

A lot of years have passed since then and I am still not a good storm walker, but I know I'll never forget whittled dolls and pine trees bending in the storm in fields where friends once walked.

New from August House Publishers: Storytellers on tape

Listening for the Crack of Dawn

Master storyteller Donald Davis recalls the Appalachia of the '50s and '60s. "His stories often left listeners limp with laughter at the same time they struggled with a lump in the throat."—Wilma Dykeman, *New York Times*
2 cassettes, 120 minutes, ISBN 0-87483-147-4, $16.95

Favorite Scary Stories of American Children

A culturally diverse collection of shivery tales gathered from kids themselves. Collected and told by Richard and Judy Dockrey Young.
2 cassettes, 60 minutes each
Part 1 (for ages 5-8): ISBN 0-87483-148-2, $9.95
Part 2 (for ages 7-10): ISBN 0-87483-175-X, $9.95

Johnny Appleseed, Gentle Hero

Marc Joel Levitt's stories of the American legend Johnny Appleseed keep history alive and teach humanitarian values to children.
1 cassette, 45 minutes, ISBN 0-87483-176-8, $9.95

Graveyard Tales

Recorded live at the National Storytelling Festival, this tape includes chilling stories from some of America's best storytellers.
1 cassette, 45 minutes, ISBN 0-879991-02-2, $9.98

Homespun Tales

A country-flavored collection of stories recorded live at the National Storytelling Festival, with signature tales by admired tellers Doc McConnell, Kathryn Windham, Donald Davis, The Folktellers, and others.
1 cassette, 50 minutes, ISBN 0-8799903-9, $9.98

Ghost Stories from the American Southwest

Shivery tales collected from people throughout the Southwest. Performed by extraordinary storytellers Richard and Judy Dockrey Young.
1 cassette, 60 minutes, ISBN 0-87483-149-0, $9.95

August House Publishers
P.O. Box 3223, Little Rock, Arkansas 72203
1-800-284-8784